The Secret Adventures of Rolo

Book 3

The Dragon's Pram

By Debi Evans

Illustrations by Chantal Bourgonje

Rolo's grammar corrected by Emma Corbett

www.debievans.com

Published by Debi Evans
First Edition published in 2015
Printed by Biddles
Blackborough End, Norfolk

ISBN 978-0-9928257-4-4

Rolo would like to give special thanks to Chantal who draws him, Emma who corrects his grammar, Michelle who gives him holidays, Gareth who trains him, the boy with the rabbit, the girl who doesn't like dogs and the floppy haired boy who undoes the training and the smiley lady who loves him most of all.

For anyone new to the series, Rolo is a rescued Jack Russell and also 'the chosen one', discovering he has the ability to time travel via a hidden passage in an oak tree whenever he brings his pink ball, under the direction of Athelstan, guardian of the forest.

Rolo travels back through history in secret and always at night, to witness and sometimes influence events - Unbeknown to his owners: the smiley lady and the floppy haired boy, who wonder why their lovable pet is often tired during the day!

Life with Rolo is a constant adventure and I am assured he has many stories to tell so there are more books to come.

You can follow him on Twitter @rolodogblog and listen to his podcasts. He also has a Facebook page 'rolodogblog' and would appreciate a 'like'!

www.debievans.com

Contents

www.debievans.com

The Secret Adventures of Rolo

Book 3

The Dragon's Pram

Prologue

Edging past the familiar plastic bucket and rubber gloves in the cupboard under the kitchen sink, I found myself feeling for the ring with my nose and with a few twists and turns I managed to open the secret trapdoor with my teeth.

Hurrying down the garden steps, I squeezed under the gate and ran along the well-worn paths until I found the right bushes around the clearing. I knew the route through the forest off by heart now and didn't hesitate, confidently heading onwards in the dark of night: no time for exploring on the way.

Lying flat I wriggled forward on my tummy and disappeared in the undergrowth. Suddenly I was right there at the foot of the Athelstan tree.

Excitement hung in the air, mixed up with the night time woody scent of damp earth and vegetation.

I gazed up, anticipating the friendly face of the dragon wrapped around the tree.

'What's the matter Little Pup? Can't you sleep?'

The kindly dragon face smiled down as he emerged from the bark of the old oak and again I wondered whether the guardian of the time tunnel was actually part of the tree.

Athelstan hadn't summoned me. No sign of the owl nor the little woodland folk. It was just the tree dragon and I, and I wanted to ask him something important.

I stood up on my back legs and leaned my front paws on the tree: my way of hugging him in greeting. Then I pressed my nose into the bark and inhaled the wonderful earthy aroma.

The dragon stirred, and the leaves echoed his movement rustling on their branches.

'You are wondering if I am a real dragon, am I right?'

Wow! How did he know that? It was as if he could read my thoughts!

'I once flew over treetops, soaring through the night on silent wings, but when the dragons disappeared I hid in this ancient forest because I wanted to stay in these woods where I felt safe and secure.

'When I discovered this tree and the secret within it, I appointed myself guardian and so as to do my job properly I wrapped my body around the trunk, and, over time, I became part of the tree. Does that satisfy your curiosity?'

9

The gentle voice and the rustling of leaves tailed off and I could imagine Athelstan smiling in the dark.

'Why did the dragons disappear?' I wondered aloud and Athelstan shook his woody face and said, quite simply,

'That's another story.'

'Are there any dragons alive today?' I asked eagerly, not wanting the discussion to end.

'Oh yes,' said Athelstan and with that, rather annoyingly, he faded into the bark.

No amount of pleading would bring another word from the tree dragon that night.

Chapter 1

Rolo and the Canal Disaster

I love the Kennet and Avon Canal. Brightly coloured barges chug up and down the 87 mile waterway and I think it would be a lovely peaceful way to travel. The smiley lady and floppy haired boy often take me for long walks along the tow paths at Hungerford, Bradford on Avon and Honey Street, but my favourite stretch of all is the Caen Hill locks at Devizes.

Athelstan sent Yulia and Bubo the owl to tell me he had a very important mission for me involving the canal.

For this adventure I would need to travel to the neighbouring market town of Devizes, where I had met the shire horses and found out about 'moonrakers' on previous adventures. The guardian dragon gave me the low down on the two hundred year old canal.

'Work had commenced on the waterway in 1794 from both ends: from Bradford on Avon west to

Bath/Bristol and east to Devizes, and from Newbury to Reading.

'The Kennet and Avon canal was an ambitious project originally planned to follow the natural contours of the land.'

I asked Athelstan how the canals were actually built as it seemed a massive engineering project to me.

'Dug out by hand, little pup. Canal builders in the 18th and 19th centuries were called 'cutters' because they literally had to cut a channel through the ground. The term 'navigators' was adopted and, from this, the more familiar 'navvies' stuck; these were casual workers made up from farm hands, ex-miners and quarrymen.' Athelstan explained.

The trickiest part of this particular canal, and the last stretch to be constructed, was the dilemma of Caen Hill in Devizes: a short steep hill. The problem had been temporarily overcome by a horse drawn rail track, but this was not ideal because the cargo had to be unloaded from the barges then horse-drawn up hill and then reloaded onto the barges at the top.

The dramatic height of the land meant a stairway of 16 locks had to be built very close to each other with the use of 'side ponds' to refill each lock after use: the brain child of engineer John Rennie. This staircase forms part of the 29 lock flight at Devizes which spans two miles. It was to this spot that Athelstan wanted to send me.

So this is how I came to find myself on Caen Hill where the steep flight of locks and ponds were under construction. It was 1810. (This was the year not the time!)

I watched for a while as physically strong bare-chested men wielded their combined muscle power to heave pick and shovel. It seemed to me the job entailed much digging and removal of surplus earth by means of nothing fancier than a wooden wheelbarrow.

It looked like tough and dangerous work with very basic tools and, listening to the men grumbling, they received very little pay for their efforts.

Re-drawing some of the plans after the work had commenced meant escalating costs: some hills needed tunnelling through because the ground was not all soft clay as originally thought, and rock had to be blasted with gunpowder.

I watched a pair of navvies larking about whilst emptying dug mud from their wooden wheelbarrow. They started flinging it about and a few others joined in.

I frowned, thinking 'this won't get the job finished'.

I looked about but there didn't seem to be anyone in charge and no one was supervising this stage of the construction. Health and safety rules seemed non-existent in the early 19th century. I thought there was supposed to be an overseer from the canal company on site but these men had been left to their own devices.

I strolled up to the top lock to see how progress was going. Perhaps I could be the foreman? I fancied myself as a project manager.

I sat on the bank and watched several men climb

down into the deep channel to test the lining to see if this last lock was dry. They were balancing rather precariously on wooden planks suspended over the canal bed so as not to damage the newly laid lining.

I remembered that Athelstan had told me that the lining was made from a mixture of local clay and loam known as 'puddle clay'. The navvies had to get this bit right or the channel would simply not be watertight.

On the side of the channel, two men were sorting big stones and marking them with their special mason mark. This local stone for constructing the sides of the canal came from the quarry down river at Bathampton.

One of the navvies, a big brawny man, suddenly glanced up and shouted at me to clear off. I suppose they didn't want me leaving any paw prints on their handiwork. I scampered out of range of the stones he was sending my way.

I ran along the bank of the canal, the part that would eventually become the tow path – so called because

15

the first barges were horse-drawn and therefore 'towed' as they had no engine.

To my surprise, in the next lock down the flight, where the puddle clay lining was almost set hard, a herd of cattle was being encouraged to go down a ramp. I couldn't figure out the purpose of this, but then thought that it was probably to help flatten the base and really pack it down tightly. The cows were reluctant to go down the ramp and the navvies didn't seem to know much about cow herding. I sat and watched this entertainment for a while – there was no way those cows were going down the ramp.

Surveying this scene, I wondered why Athelstan had sent me here, and then I heard a slight creak.

Well, it started more as a 'groan' than a 'creak', and I ran to the top overflow pond where I thought the sound was coming from.

The creak got louder and was followed by an ominous rumble.

I could see at once what was happening: the weight of the water was going to force open the lock gate and the men investigating the lining had no way of getting out once that volume of water started gushing in!

I had to act quickly.

'Not you again! Get away!' shouted the big man with tattoos on his muscular arms, as he looked up and scowled at me from the bottom of the lock.

I started yapping and barking more and more insistently, jumping around in circles: I had to get them to realise the danger they were in, but this wasn't working!

I looked around frantically, desperate for a way to attract their attention and spied a lunch pack tied up with string lying beside the tow path. I snatched it up and started running. That did the trick! No labourer would want to lose his lunch!

The men started to climb the steel-rung ladder up the sheer stone wall of the canal in pursuit of the stolen food. Their shouts masked the creaks of the straining lock. As the last navvy had his foot on the bottom rung, the sluice gate could no longer hold back the force of goodness knows how many gallons of water and the dam burst open. The water level started to rise rapidly right to the top of the canal. A moment longer on the bottom of the dry lock and they would have all drowned.

I held my breath as the last man managed to stay one rung ahead of the water. All the men were now safely on the tow path and couldn't believe their lucky escape. No one had even got their boots wet.

Thank goodness the cows in the next lock had refused to go down the ramp, or they would have perished in the mass of water which was taking no prisoners as it flooded down the new flight of locks.

I was rewarded with a hunk of bread and ham from the lunch pack I had stolen, which I wolfed down in seconds, and then succumbed to a lot of rough petting. The big man crouched down and ruffled my ears as he called me 'Boyo' – he must have been from my native Wales.

Sharing their lunch and looking at the canal construction, I had an idea which I needed to share with them so that they would hopefully never be in this kind of dangerous situation again.

For some reason I couldn't communicate with these men like I can with some humans when I time travel. Instead, I had to demonstrate my idea. I went over to a plank of wood and nudged it over on its side, leaning it against two big stones for support.

'What is this daft mutt doing?' queried one of the navvies. They all watched, baffled.

'Ah, I get it, you clever dog!' said the Welshman,

'We cut slots, see, in the sides of the feeder locks, so if ever we need to stop the water flow to inspect or make repairs, we can slide a plank of wood in and temporarily isolate the lock which needs repair.' The men agreed it was a brilliant idea. That would be mine, then.

I learned from Athelstan, later, that the success of the Kennet and Avon canal was short-lived because of the coming of the railway to the region.

In 1852, just forty years later, the great engineer Isambard Kingdom Brunel's Great Western Railway Company bought up the canal company very cheaply and soon railway replaced waterway, as it was a more efficient form of transportation for goods.

For now, my mission was complete and I went home with tail wagging, pleased about the lives I had saved.

I will always have a wry smile on my furry face when I walk along the Kennet and Avon canal with

20

my people in future. I wonder if they will notice the slots for the planks by the lock gates – my idea.

Back to my basket with a full tummy and the luxury of sleep.

Dog blog #1 - According to Rolo

The smiley lady likes a general knowledge crossword in Saturday's newspaper because she says it keeps her mind active.

She had gone to church on Sunday morning and I thought I would have a look at yesterday's crossword puzzle and see if she needed any help. I jumped up on the dining room table with the aid of a chair that hadn't been pushed in properly. This was daring stuff as I knew jolly well I wasn't allowed up there. She seemed to be stuck on a few, though; let's see...

3 down: female swan. She'd written in 'cob' and then tried to rub it out. I knew the correct term was 'pen'…but where had she put her pen? I couldn't find anything to write the answer with.

I heard the key turn in the front door lock and froze to the spot as the door opened and she had almost caught me up on the table doing her crossword puzzle. To create a diversion I picked up her reading glasses and jumped down, running towards her carrying them gently in my mouth.

'Oh, Rolo, what on earth are you doing with my glasses? Have you been trying to finish my crossword?' She tried to sound cross about me being on the table, but I could tell that she secretly found it

The Secret Adventures of Rolo

funny. In the end I saw her look up
the answer to 3 down. ☺

Chapter 2

Rolo and the Welsh Dragon

'Are you still thinking about dragons, Little Pup?' Athelstan asked me a few nights later.

'I've been dreaming about them,' I replied truthfully, no longer surprised that the guardian dragon was able to read my mind.

'Have you still got that collar Father Christmas gave you when you helped him sort out his reindeer problem last year? You need to fetch it here.'

I remembered the new collar with the shiny crystal mounted in it. I wore it proudly on Christmas Day and now it hung in the utility room as a spare collar, because the smiley lady was afraid I might lose the crystal.

The next day, when the smiley lady was busy in the garden and the floppy haired boy was at school, I went into the utility room and saw the collar hanging on a peg. How was I going to be able to reach it, though?

There was a stool close by that the smiley lady used to stand on when she needed to reach things from the top of the cupboard.

That should do it.

I nudged the stool across the floor with my nose and scrambled up. Standing on my hind legs, with my front paws leaning on the coats, I could just about reach the collar.

I had to balance for a moment and then quickly knock it down with my right forepaw. Then I jumped down onto the tiled floor and hid the collar in my basket in the kitchen before anyone noticed it and possibly hung it back up on the hook.

That night when everyone was asleep, I took the

collar to Athelstan, carrying it carefully in my mouth.

'That will do the job,' said the ancient tree dragon, mysteriously.

Athelstan started making a very strange keening sound, as if he were in pain. I wasn't sure what to do, but he lifted his fore-claw to his lips as if to shush me, and then he turned his head up to the sky and made the dreadful noise again.

I sat very still on the forest floor with my feet gathered in, one ear up and my head on one side, wondering what might happen next.

Absolutely nothing.

Silence…and then, a whoosh of wind and a great beating of wings and I darted behind the oak tree, terrified of whatever monster Athelstan had conjured up.

'Bore Dar,' said Athelstan to the silhouette of the winged stranger by way of greeting.

'Bore Dar,' came the reply, in a creaky voice which made me think of old leather.

It sounded a bit like Athelstan's voice but with more of an accent. I couldn't see who the speaker was, so I edged around the tree and peered hard into the darkness from the safety of the tree roots. I knew that word from my puppyhood and knew it was a Welsh greeting.

Before I could say anything, I heard Yulia's tiny voice pipe up,

'Rhydian! Is that really you?'

The creature with its back to me settled down on its haunches and Yulia clambered over the tree root, ran up to it and stroked its nose.

'Cariad,' it said.

I remember Yulia doing that to me the first time we met.

The creaky voice made a sound a bit like the purring of – dare I say – a cat. It seemed content and perhaps

27

not as dangerous as it first appeared.

'Little Pup, don't be afraid! Come and meet Rhydian, he doesn't bite,' Athelstan encouraged, and added,

'Though he may scorch,' with a glint of amusement in his beady eyes.

The creature turned his head in my direction and I could see the scales glistening in the moonlight.

Rhydian was a truly magnificent red dragon with a golden sheen giving him a sort of other-worldly quality.

I crouched down beside Yulia and she reached up to fondle my ear.

Rhydian smiled a dragony smile and I wondered if perhaps he might be related to Athelstan, although he was a different colour. He was staring at the crystal on the collar, now lying on the tree roots where I had left it.

Yulia picked the collar up and fastened it around my neck with some difficulty: with her being so tiny she had to clamber over me to fix it in place. The dragon watched with interest. Yulia whispered to me,

'Dragons are attracted by shiny objects. They love jewels. See how Rhydian can't take his eyes off your collar?'

'He can have it!' I murmured nervously from the corner of my mouth and backing away slightly. I didn't like the way the dragon was staring at me.

'No, not yet,' whispered Yulia, 'he must give you something in exchange.' She put a restraining arm on my paw.

'Such as?' I wondered aloud.

'What are you two whispering about?' spoke up Athelstan, silencing us both at once.

'Brave Pup, you said you wanted to see a real dragon and here you are, I've summoned one for you. Rhydian is the only remaining Welsh dragon.'

'Ci Em,' said Rhydian, bowing his head slightly towards me. My knowledge of Welsh vocabulary

29

had run out and I thought this was some kind of greeting, but didn't know how to respond. He then added,

'Not quite.'

'How do you do,' I said nervously. I was a bit concerned that the dragon might be hungry and that he might consider me a tasty little snack, but I forgot that dragons can read thoughts, and both dragons burst out laughing and Yulia joined in too.

'In exchange for the crystal on your collar, Rhydian will take you for a flight. Would you like to fly on a dragon?' Athelstan asked, kindly.

I was both nervous and excited at the same time and at once, quite involuntarily, started the terrier shake.

Yulia stroked my nose again. I felt calmer but my heart was pounding. The red dragon and the tree dragon were deep in conversation and I couldn't understand what they were saying.

I was sure that Athelstan wouldn't send me off with this winged creature if there was any danger at all of me becoming his lunch.

Athelstan turned to me and spoke,

'I'm not sure if you know this, but dragons can time travel…Perhaps you would like to go back to the Iron Age when dragons were a bit more visible? Rhydian has a job to do and he needs your help.'

I nodded, and then whispered to Athelstan,

'What does Ci Em mean?'

'Jewel dog,' the tree dragon said simply.

Then the pantomime began. How was I going to get on this dragon's back?

Rhydian crouched down low and sprawled out like a rug, trying to lie flat on the ground, inviting me with a grunt to climb up on his back. I'm pretty good at jumping and we dogs don't take a run-up like a human attempting a high jump. Instead we flex our muscles and bend our knees and then jump from a stationary position.

I knew, without even trying, that the height of the

The Secret Adventures of Rolo

dragon's back was beyond my short terrier legs.

Athelstan said something to Rhydian in an old language I didn't understand, and the red dragon crawled closer to the oak tree and again spread out flat, as close to the ground as he could but this time lying in a ditch on the other side of the tree.

I realised at once what Athelstan meant for me to do and I climbed carefully over the tree roots which gave me a height advantage. It was easier to climb down onto the scaly back, and this worked.

I wrapped my front paws tightly around Rhydian's neck as he harrumphed and made an attempt to get up on his feet. In order to gain his full height, the dragon was a bit like a camel, going up on his back knees first and then suddenly rocking forward to transfer his weight – with such a jolt that he nearly unseated me. Finally he came to standing. I was mighty high up and clinging on for dear life!

Gripping the dragon with my knees like a jockey on a racehorse, Rhydian asked me if we were ready to go.

I woofed my assent and he increased his pace from walk to run, stumbling and tripping over the brambles and branches on the forest floor.

Suddenly my magnificent red flying machine was flapping his massive wings and we were at once airborne with me clinging round his neck and my ears billowing behind me.

At first we stayed quite close to the ground, brushing over the undergrowth and weaving in and out of the tall trees. Then we came to a clearing and Rhydian seemed to step up a gear.

When I felt brave enough to look down at the ground, I saw the trees of the forest below us, and then roads, cars and houses looking like a tiny

33

model village getting smaller and smaller as we gained height.

I was starting to enjoy this flight and relaxed my grip, finding my balance and imagining I was seated on a magic carpet.

We soared higher and higher and were eventually above the clouds. It was much colder up here.

I don't have a great sense of direction, but it seemed to me that we were making a great big figure of eight shape in the sky. We rose high and soared low as we completed the loop back to the point where we had started, and then we came below the clouds again as the dragon dipped his wings.

It seemed this was the end of the roller-coaster ride.

Chapter 3

Rolo in the Iron Age

As we started our descent, I looked around for the familiar roads that led to the forest but I could see no trees at all, just vast plains.

Funny, because I really believed that we were coming back to land in the place we had started from.

'I know what you're thinking, Ci Em,' said Rhydian as he touched down for a landing smoother than any airplane.

'You are right in your logical thinking – we are back in exactly the same spot geographically but about 2500 years earlier. It is not yet a forest. Look about you and tell me what you see.'

I stayed on the dragons back, afraid to get off because if I dismounted here I couldn't see how I would be able to climb back up and I certainly didn't want to be stuck in this barren era! Whatever would the smiley lady do without me?

I reported that I could see vast plains of nothingness; there really was not a lot to see. I knew that some of the trees in the forest dated back about 1000 years, but was there really nothing here prior to that?

Rhydian said to hold tight and took me on a short, low-level flight a few miles further west – as the dragon flies. He homed in on a slight hill, which appeared from above to resemble one of those children's skill puzzles where you tip the silver balls around the 'maze' very gently to encourage them to settle in different holes whilst you carefully line them all up.

We alighted on the ground near the hill. Rhydian told me that this was Windmill Hill, thought to be the site of the first settlement at Avebury. I have been here for walks with the smiley lady in present time.

'What is it used for?' I asked the dragon as we watched people walking towards the hill from all directions, 'Why are they coming here?' my natural curiosity was bursting.

'It is a kind of meeting place,' said Rhydian. 'The

people come here to trade animals, celebrate births, pairings and also to commemorate death. They also celebrate the changing seasons, realising that the weather plays a huge part in the success of their crops and the health of their livestock from year to year.'

Rhydian was warming to his subject,

'People who learn about history in the 21st century think that when the Romans invaded Britain, they found the indigenous Celtic people to be quite primitive, without much going on in their lives, and they truly believe that Roman influence could only have benefited them. How wrong they are to believe that!

'This was a period of time which spanned several hundreds of years and saw many changes. That is why these different eras are called 'Stone Age', 'Iron Age' and 'Bronze Age', depending on which resources were discovered and used. These 'ages' existed at roughly the same time all over the area we now call Europe.'

Extraordinary! I thought.

He stopped for a moment to gather his thoughts and I couldn't think of anything intelligent to say so I stayed silent. He went on,

'Historians in modern times make assumptions about the Ancient Britons because there is no written account of life surviving from that time, but the evidence is there in other forms, hidden away under the ground.

'Heavy rain in a field over a period of time can sometimes yield secrets from the past such as flint heads, proving ancient military presence, or cooking pots showing metal work knowledge. Culture didn't start with the Romans.

'Inhabitants of pre-Roman Britain already knew how to spin, weave, grind corn, rear livestock and grow crops. They built dwelling places, practised some kind of religion and also travelled, and they defended their settlements by constructing hill forts and henges.

'Who were these Ancient Britons and where did

they come from?' I asked.

'This area of the South West of Britain was probably settled by people coming from Northern Europe from about 500BC onwards, attracted by its warm climate. They travelled in large tribes and fought with each other as they journeyed, to claim and settle the land they found along the way.'

I asked Rhydian about hill forts as I knew from Athelstan they were a surviving feature from this time.

I listened to Rhydian's soft creaky voice as he told me there were more than a thousand hill forts constructed in England and Wales.

A hill fort was a simple means of defence: a hill with a ditch dug around it and the earth from the ditch would be piled up in a bank on one side. Along the top of the bank people would use either sharpened wooden stakes, or else a stone wall to strengthen the defence. Whenever danger was sensed, villagers would flock to the hill fort taking their possessions and even their cattle inside for safety.

When Rhydian stopped speaking, I told him everything I knew about the Amesbury Archer and my adventure in the Bronze Age, which was of course in the future.

The dragon nodded wisely, and I hoped he was impressed with my knowledge. When conversation petered out, our full attention returned to the events unfolding in front of us. I had a good vantage point from high up on the dragon's back.

It looked as if this was going to be quite a large gathering of people and, judging by the number of fires that were being prepared and tripods being erected, this hungry crowd were expecting to be fed.

I watched in fascination as a dozen large iron cauldrons were carried and hung over fires and freshly slaughtered deer were being skinned by womenfolk in their clothing made from animal pelts. The fresh meat was divided between the cooking pots along with armfuls of leaves I presumed to be herbs to add seasoning.

These Celts may have fought amongst themselves

over the right to hunt or farm a particular piece of land, but they also enjoyed getting together for a feast. Celtic blacksmiths made iron tools that could work the heavy soil and therefore they could grow better crops than their predecessors.

Rhydian pointed out some pits that had been dug to store wheat and barley after summer harvesting for use throughout the winter.

There were fenced enclosures made of woven branches, known as wattle, and wood to contain pigs, cattle, goats and sheep, shared between the round huts which made up a village.

Each hut had an earth bank and ditch around it, marking its territory. Beer was brewed and drunk from earthen pots, and grain was ground between stones to make flour and then bread.

I recognised turnips, parsnips, cabbages and beans being prepared by the womenfolk with their sharp knives, and watched them being added to the cooking pots.

A funny thought crossed my mind: that the floppy

41

haired boy didn't like any of these vegetables! He wouldn't last long in the Iron Age – no sign of broccoli, frozen peas or sweetcorn! – These are also my favourite vegetables by the way.

The smell of the aromatic meat rose as it started to cook and it filled our nostrils. I could sense that Rhydian was getting hungry too.

This was to be a victory feast. We worked out, from observing what was going on, that the brave warriors from recent battles were being feted, which meant that neighbouring tribes were getting together to add their congratulations. The heroes were brought gifts and would enjoy the best of the meat from the cooking pots.

Warriors were top of the village hierarchy and their deeds were sung about by bards (poets and musicians), who were rated next in importance, followed by the craftsmen, landowners, farmers, servants and last of all the slaves.

I caught a glimpse of a man in a brightly coloured heavy woven cloak fastened with a pin and wearing a dagger in his belt. Rhydian said he was the chief of the tribe.

Religious matters were taken care of by the Druids and we saw a few in their flowing robes. In those days religion, law and history were all closely linked. The dead were always buried with items which might be of use in the afterlife and this continued into the Bronze Age as I already knew.

I shifted my weight on Rhydian's back. I'd been sitting still for so long that I felt I was getting a 'dead leg'.

The dragon responded to my fidgeting. Our shuffling did not go unnoticed. I had just been thinking how strange it was that none of these Celts had given us a second glance – perhaps they were used to seeing dragons? Or maybe we were invisible? But I thought too soon…

A child spotted us and shouted. Suddenly people turned in our direction and started pointing at us.

The man we had identified as being the chief lifted an animal horn from his belt to his bearded lips and

blew a long and mournful note.

The noise of the assembled crowd increased like a giant wave as panic spread. The warriors, whose party we were spoiling, picked up their weapons and started making terrible war cries in our general direction.

I wondered at first if this was part of the entertainment for the feast and then quickly realised by their fierce demeanour that they were coming right at us. The women and children were scampering towards the hill fort, knocking cooking pots over into the fires and spilling the contents in their hurry to obey the command to flee.

44

The Secret Adventures of Rolo

'Time to leave the Iron Age, Ci Em, but there is something I have to do here before we return to your century.'

Rhydian knew we were in immediate danger and I hung on around his neck with my front paws as we took to the air once more.

I was sorry that we had caused alarm and broken up the feast, but it didn't seem as if the Celts were in the mood to welcome strangers, especially large red fire-breathing ones!

Three giant strides and we were airborne. A few stones were fired from slings and a couple of long spears glanced off Rhydian's thick scales as we gained height, but we were thankfully soon out of range.

I was tired out from my adventure and tried hard not to fall asleep as I clung to the dragon's straining neck, thinking about what had suddenly alerted the humans to our presence.

Suddenly I was wide awake again as we came to a halt with a jolt, not in the 21st century forest but at the entrance to a cave. What on earth had Rhydian in store for me now I wondered?

He told me to lie flat as we were going into the cave and the ceiling was quite low. I obediently lay down along his back and avoided banging my head.

'I need you to look after something for me, Ci Em,' the red dragon spoke softly and breathed gentle flames into the cave to illuminate the interior.

We were heading for the darkest corner of the cave. I peered around in the half light and spied a pile of leaves and moss. It looked very much like a giant nest. Rhydian was making a gentle crooning sound as we approached and using his fore claw he carefully moved aside the covering to reveal a pearlescent glow within. More scraping and crooning followed and his gentle movements soon revealed a very large glowing egg. I stared at it, wondering what sort of creature it might contain.

'I can't keep this dragon egg secret for much longer and soon will come the hatching. Will you take it back to your era for me?'

'Well I would,' I replied at once, 'but Athelstan said we can't bring live creatures from the past into the 21st century,' remembering Flint, the Bronze Age dog who wanted to follow me into the time tunnel.

'I have already cleared this with Athelstan – as long as we transport the egg before it hatches, otherwise it will be impossible.' Rhydian paused and took a deep breath,

'Well, Ci Em, can you do this for Athelstan and for all dragon kind?'

All sorts of thoughts were racing through my little doggy brain. I doubted Rhydian could make any sense of them because they were bouncing around

47

inside my head like frozen peas spilled on the floor from the top drawer of the freezer. How could I keep this dragon egg secret from the smiley lady and the floppy haired boy? Where would I keep it? What do I do when it hatches? How long have we got until the hatching? What do baby dragons eat?

'Don't worry, Ci Em, you will not be alone, you have Athelstan and the woodland folk to help you. Say you'll do it and we'll transport the egg this minute. Not a moment to lose. It's too dangerous to keep here any longer with the Celts and Britons ranging far and wide to hunt – it's only a matter of time before this cave is discovered. They would take the egg and goodness knows what would happen. They might break it and not allow it to hatch, fearing and not understanding what creature is contained within.'

It was a powerful and persuasive speech. I was still up on Rhydian's back so I couldn't see the pleading expression on his scaly face, but I could hear the urgency in his voice and knew I had to help him save this dragon.

Rhydian knew he'd won me over without me having to say anything. He picked up the large egg very gently in his mouth, which meant that the lights in the cave suddenly went out.

I forgot to duck as we exited the cave and banged my head on the low ceiling, but it wasn't serious and I kept my balance. Once more we were airborne with no conversation this time as the dragon was carrying the precious cargo in his powerful jaws.

I slept, dreaming of dragons again.

I woke with a start when Rhydian touched down on the forest floor and emptied his mouth gently at the foot of the Athelstan tree. Immediately Yulia and Da were there, covering the egg with a pile of last year's leaf mould and moss to keep it safe and warm. I had the feeling that they might have done this before.

'You have done well, Little Pup,' the creaky voice of Athelstan could be heard as he leant down to inspect the heap.

'Off to bed with you now before your empty basket is discovered. You are going to have to look after the

49

egg as it can't stay here. Bring your little friend with you tomorrow night – I have a feeling you might need some help!'

I found myself back in my basket before morning, and lay there wondering how it had been possible to time travel on a dragon's back without going through the tunnel in the oak tree.

Perhaps it had something to do with swooping high over the clouds and dipping low in a figure of eight, crossing some invisible time threshold. I couldn't work it out at all – and what was all that about a dragon egg? Was I really going to become a dragon's nursemaid? Did I really bring it back with me or had I simply imagined the whole adventure and not been anywhere at all? I eventually drifted off to sleep.

After breakfast, the smiley lady and I were out in the fields, and who should come bounding towards us but my little friend Chickpea.

The small Jack Russell greeted me in the usual way, ambushing me on the footpath by jumping out from the bushes, before we went through the usual routine of dancing around each other and sniffing both ends.

'Chickpea, am I glad to see you!' I whispered when my face was level with her ear.

'I need your help with moving something. We need some kind of small cart or a vehicle with wheels at any rate.'

Our owners had already discussed the weather and were now heading in opposite directions. Luckily Chickpea was quite quick in catching on with the transport request.

'Forest. Tonight,' I barked as we went our separate ways on the field. She trotted off with her tail high, waving like a flag. I hoped she could find what was needed. I could only lay my paws on a skateboard and I didn't think that would be very suitable.

Dog blog #2 - According to Rolo

After we'd left Chickpea, we carried on down the hill to the newsagents. The smiley lady bent down to tie my lead to the railing. She doesn't usually like to leave me outside a shop because she knows I hate being left and also she's afraid that someone might try to dognap me.

Silly smiley lady unclipped the lead from my collar and tied it to the post but forgot to reattach it to me. I knew what she wanted, so I ran inside the shop as someone was coming out, and headed over to the newspaper section. If she had given me the money I could have bought one for her as I know which one she likes to read: the one with the crossword.

Instead she came running into the shop after me all out of breath and grabbed me by the collar and marched me back outside, much to

the amusement of the staff. I don't
know what all the fuss was about.
According to the sign on the door
it's only Scottie dogs that are not
allowed to enter shops. ☺

Back home, after a good brushing, I
came indoors and pushed the door of
the utility room open with my nose
and glanced up at the peg where
my special Christmas collar was
kept. I got up on my back legs for
a better look and sure enough, the

53

collar was back up there but the crystal was missing. I don't even remember returning to my basket the previous night, nor hanging the collar on its hook, but I was sure that Rhydian had taken the crystal in payment for my adventure, just as Yulia said he would.

But, boy oh boy, had he given ME something in exchange!

Chapter 4

The Dragon's Pram

That night, without being summoned, I took myself to the Athelstan tree. A glance at the piled heap at the foot of it reassured me that the egg was real and not a figment of my imagination.

I hoped that Chickpea had understood the urgency of my whispered message.

Whilst we were waiting for her I asked Athelstan something that had been puzzling me ever since I had met Rhydian,

'I remember once overhearing the floppy haired boy telling the smiley lady that the English used to have a white dragon as their symbol on their flag. Is that right?'

Athelstan unfurled himself from the tree trunk and bent his face down close to talk to me.

'A history lesson for you, Little Pup: Hengist and Horsa were brothers who landed in Britain with other Angles, Saxons and Jutes in the early 400s to fight for Vortigern, the then King of Britain. Hengist went on to rule the Anglo Saxons for a period of around 30 years.

'His symbol was that of a white dragon, and when his army went to fight against the people of 'Wiales' ('strangers', now called Wales) it was true that the red and the white dragons would actually meet in combat, and I don't just mean their pictures on their battle flags.'

I tried to take this in but didn't really know what Athelstan meant.

Whilst the tree dragon was talking I kept glancing down at the heap of leaves, trying to detect any signs of movement which would surely mean new dragon life.

Reading my thoughts, Athelstan said,

'It's too cold for the egg outdoors in the forest. It needs to be kept at a constant temperature for the next few weeks.'

'What happened to the white dragon then, if it was a real dragon and not just a picture on a flag?' I asked, returning my gaze to the tree dragon and keen to know more.

'Perhaps he is still here,' said Athelstan mysteriously and then retreated into the bark.

'Tell me when your little friend is here,' said the voice as it faded.

Hmmm. Food for thought. I had heard the smiley lady say that the white dragon flag was proudly carried into battle at the head of an English army right up until the 11th century by the Kings of Wessex. I wondered why it wasn't used anymore.

A curious sound of creaking broke into my thoughts and I saw Chickpea wriggle through the undergrowth pushing something that looked very much like a doll's pram.

'Will this do?' asked Chickpea, struggling with the exertion of pushing the thing all the way from her home.

'I think it's perfect!' I said, impressed with the little terrier.

'I found it in the garage – it belongs to my people but I don't think they play with it anymore. What do we need it for?' she asked eagerly.

Yulia and Da held up their lanterns, illuminating the heap of leaves at the base of the tree. Athelstan revealed himself again.

'Oh goody, are we having a bonfire?' squeaked Chickpea.

'Goodness gracious, no, fires aren't allowed in the

forest in any case,' admonished the tree dragon, leaning down to survey the scene.

Yulia and Da set their lanterns on the ground and motioned to Chickpea to bring the old pram nearer to the heap.

The woodland folk gently scraped away the leaf mould and revealed the glistening egg. Chickpea's eyes were as round as dinner bowls at this amazing sight.

I explained in hushed tones about the dragon egg and how I'd brought it from the Iron Age and that it couldn't stay in the forest because it wasn't warm enough to hatch and also there was a big risk of it getting broken.

'Where are we going to take it then?' asked Chickpea, all ears.

'My house,' I said a bit louder, for the benefit of the assembled woodland audience.

'I've found the perfect hiding place – in the airing cupboard. It's hardly ever used and I had a look in there when I was exploring upstairs and there's a pile of old towels and bathmats on the floor in there. We could tuck the egg up behind the hot water tank. That would be very snug. In fact I wouldn't mind sleeping in there myself!'

Yulia giggled. 'You won't have to hatch the egg yourself, Rolo!'

'Of course not, I know that!' I said.

'I thought your people had a stair gate to stop you going upstairs? How will you be able to access the airing cupboard?' said Chickpea.

'They took it down and said I was to be trusted now because I am a good boy,' I answered with a smirk. She didn't say anything to this, remembering having her 'cat flap' locked for a while after she went missing during a previous adventure.

'It will make a perfect incubator, but you will just have to keep an eye on the temperature,' said Athelstan, 'don't let it get too hot or too cold. You can add or remove towels as necessary.'

Everybody helped to line the pram with moss and leaves to stop the egg from being damaged during transit. The old doll's pram had very little in the way of suspension and I feared the egg may be in for a bumpy ride.

All we had to do now was transfer the egg into its pram. But how were we going to do that? We all stood around looking at each other.

Athelstan suggested that Yulia and Da hold on to the pram wheels and he directed Chickpea and I to very carefully manoeuvre the egg with our front paws, lifting it up and then laying it back down gently onto its mossy bed in the borrowed pram.

We managed to accomplish this delicate task without too much fuss, but we did squabble all the way home, fighting over whose turn it was to push the pram and blaming each other when the egg bounced alarmingly every time the pram wheel caught a tree root or went down a pot hole.

Miraculously we reached my garden. New challenge: how on earth were we going to get the pram through the garden gate? It certainly wouldn't fit underneath it which was of course my usual point of entry.

'Wait there,' Chickpea instructed, and she squeezed under the gate and into my garden.

'I thought so!' she said when she poked her nose back under the gate on the forest side. 'There's an old trampoline at the bottom of your garden in the nettles. If we push it over here I can jump up and open the gate.'

Sometimes Chickpea can be annoyingly clever.

We managed to shift the small trampoline between us – it was more robust than the dragon egg - and, sure enough, Chickpea bounced high a few times and worked away at the bolt with every bounce up in the air.

The egg lay quite oblivious to the drama, snug in its pram.

Eventually the bolt gave way and the gate swung open.

'We'd better put the trampoline back in the nettles in case we need it again,' I said, and we collided in our eagerness to push the pram into the sanctuary of the garden.

I was dreading seeing the floppy haired boy appear at his bedroom window!

'You will need to come into the house with me

63

Chickpea and help me through the trapdoor, because I don't think I am able to manage on my own,' I said, as I hadn't really thought about the next stage of the plan.

How on earth was I going to get the egg upstairs?

I couldn't really tell as it was still dark, but I could imagine that Chickpea was smiling, pleased to be a necessary part of this secret adventure.

We left the doll's pram in the back garden on the decking and pondered how to get the egg up the steps. I told Chickpea to wait whilst I went into the kitchen to see if there was anything on hand that might help.

I had a brainwave: I tugged down the tea towel from its hook above the radiator and went back through the trapdoor with it in my mouth.

We stood on step immediately above the pram and snuggled the egg into the tea towel with our front paws and then grabbed two opposite corners each in our teeth and carefully came up the garden steps. I gave Chickpea my corners whilst I backed into

64

the cupboard under the sink and when Chickpea followed me in and tried to pass me the precious egg I nearly dropped it in the bucket whilst we were trying to both fit in the cupboard. I told her I would go first and so I stepped down onto the kitchen floor.

I held the egg in the tea towel cradle whilst Chickpea got down. Next problem was how to open the kitchen door.

Chickpea had already thought of that. We laid the egg in its sling carefully on the floor. She stood on my shoulders and reached up to open the door handle. If she slipped she would surely land on the egg!

We paused to listen but thankfully all was quiet upstairs. I didn't even know what the time was but judging by the creeping light we didn't have long to complete our task before the smiley lady woke up.

'How on earth are we going to manage the stairs?' whispered Chickpea voicing the next hurdle we would encounter.

'Same procedure. You go backwards this time. Very

65

slowly up the stairs with the egg cradled in the sling between us. Are you ready?' I tried to sound confident.

I'm not entirely sure how, but our cunning plan worked. The airing cupboard was just at the top of the stairs and I had already thought to pull out a bit of bath mat to wedge the door slightly open so it would be easier to quietly open the door of this makeshift hidey hole.

We lay the egg on the landing carpet and set about making a nest in its new incubator. We worked quietly using our front paws to arrange the towels behind the hot water tank, and I kept an ear up in case we disturbed the sleeping inhabitants of the house.

Satisfied with our nesting, we gently laid the egg, still on the tea towel, on the bed of towels and banked up the other linen, covering the egg over and using our back legs to push the door against the bath mat until the airing cupboard was almost shut.

'That should do it,' I whispered, pleased with our

handiwork.

We silently crept downstairs. Chickpea ran home.

I forgot all about the doll's pram.

The floppy haired boy nearly tripped over it the next morning.

'Mum, there's a doll's pram on the decking!'

Dog Blog #3 - According to Rolo

The smiley lady keeps asking me why I am sitting at the bottom of the stairs. I'd have to be more careful or I'd alert her suspicion!

I just wanted to keep guard.

Athelstan assured me that nothing would happen to the egg for a few more weeks at constant temperature so I didn't need to worry just yet.

67

I reluctantly tore myself away from my sentry post and trotted into the hall at the sound of the jangling lead.

On our way out for walkies we passed the bus stop used by the children to travel to the local schools. A P.E. bag lay forlornly on the grass, quite forgotten by its owner, and the bus was probably already dropping off the children at school by now.

I sniffed the drawstring bag and pushed my nose into the opening at the top. I recognised it at once as belonging to a young lad who walks past the house every day and always says hello to me by name. I picked the bag up in my teeth and the smiley lady looked at the logo and said,

'Well, we know which school the owner goes to — we can walk that way and deliver it straight away, hopefully reuniting it with its owner before the clothes are needed for a P.E. lesson.'

I trotted ahead contentedly on my lead. I like to do good turns for people.

Soon we reached the gate. The sign on the school door says 'no dogs allowed' underneath a picture of a Scottie dog, so I don't think it applies to me. Anyway, I've been into this school before. One of the ladies from the office opened the front door to let us in.

'Oh hello, Rolo!' she said.

'What brings you to our school?

Have you come to be read to by our children?'

What a great idea that was, I thought. That would certainly get children reading!

The smiley lady explained that I had found a P.E. bag by the bus stop and the office lady bent down and patted me on the head and asked me if I knew who it belonged to. The smiley lady unclipped my lead and I trotted off down the corridor to find the little boy called Harry in year 3, whose class were about to go and get changed into their P.E. kits.

He was surprised and very pleased to see me carrying his bag in my mouth. I set it down at his feet and stretched up to give him a hug.

I don't think he'd even realised
he'd left it at the bus stop!
'That's boys for you — and also
it's the end of term and all their
heads are full of wool,' laughed
the lady from the office and the
smiley lady joined in the laughter
as she clipped my lead back on,
no doubt thinking about the floppy
haired boy.

I was trying to picture children
with woolly heads.

Dog Blog #4 - According to Rolo

One fine morning at the end of the Easter holidays, I heard the smiley lady talking about going on a journey. I panicked about the egg — this was not a good time to be going away from home!

Consulting Athelstan, he reassured me that we still had at least another week or so until the hatching and he thought it would be a good idea because the egg didn't actually need anything in its present state and, with the house being quiet, it would be completely undisturbed. Chickpea could always go in through the trapdoor and check on the temperature anyway.

Most of the children had gone back to school, and so it seemed it was a perfect time to travel.

Without too much fuss the smiley
lady bundled me and some bags into
the car and off we went in a south
westerly direction. She had packed
my bed and my doggie bowl and food
box so I knew we weren't just going
on a day trip. I settled down in
my doggy travelling cage whilst she
sang along to Radio 2.

'Are we there yet?' I wondered,
several times, poking my head up.
Finally we were.

She parked the car near a little
collection of stone buildings,
perhaps once a farm and I read the
sign, 'Old Lanwarnick'.
She let me out of the car. We
went through a small wooden gate,
crossed an enclosed gravelled

terrace and she opened the door of something called 'Spice Barn'. What a dear little cottage!

This was to be our home for the next week.

The first thing I saw was a tiled-floor lounge and through-kitchen, perfect for skittering on.

There's a big black leather sofa which I don't appear to be allowed on, and a lovely red looped rug on the floor which is great to snuggle on. The stair gate is apparently to keep me upstairs, and the smiley lady took her case and disappeared downstairs to her basket. Later we set out to explore the grounds.

Old Lanwarnick is a collection of converted farm buildings. It has a fabulous woodland walk and the primroses are out so it's particularly pretty at the moment. The winding paths lead through the woods, which used to be a quarry, and down to a stream to splash and play in. There are little wooden bridges over muddy areas, and someone has carved seats and mushrooms. It is a truly magical dell and to me, with all its exciting scents and trails, it really is a doggy adventure playground!

The Secret Adventures of Rolo

In another wooden building which looked like a former stable there is a hot tub. The smiley lady is very excited by this discovery and put on her swimsuit. The barn is partially open so you can watch the night sky whilst you relax in the soothing bubbles. Another place I'm not allowed to go. ☹

When the smiley lady disappeared down the stairs in the evening shutting the gate firmly behind her, I was a bit concerned about the strange gurgling noises coming from below.

She told me later it was a whirlpool bath and I wasn't allowed down to see that either so I'll have to take her word for it and sit quietly waiting for her to

The Secret Adventures of Rolo

reappear smelling lovely and clean and ready to snuggle.

The owners of the cottage had thoughtfully left home-baked doggy biscuits made from exciting ingredients such as pork and apple, chicken and red pepper and lamb and mint - I read the label — and fresh scones and jam and clotted cream. Apparently only the doggy biscuits were for me. ☹

Day 1
The next morning we drove along the steep and narrow lanes almost brushing the primroses, and walked around the picturesque fishing town of Looe.

We went to a friendly café on the Harbour and I liked it because I was given a bit of sausage and a

77

drink by the kindly owners whilst
the smiley lady had coffee. I had a
growling match with a seagull and
had my nose nipped by a pincer when
I peered into a bucket of wriggling
crabs which some children had
caught by dangling bits of bacon on
string from the quay. They assured
the smiley lady that they throw
back everything they catch before
they go home. Personally I think
they should paint numbers on the
crab shells, and then it would be a
bit like 'hook a duck' and children
could see which the 'greediest
crab' was. Just a thought.

The smiley lady keeps saying
'arrrr' and looking for a man in a
tricorn hat called Poldark.

I wondered at first what she was
on about, but then realised that

The Secret Adventures of Rolo

she was thinking of the Sunday night television drama, involving a Cornish copper mine and filmed around here. I watch it with her because there is a dog in it. I like television programmes with dogs in. This one is particularly handsome but doesn't need great acting ability as it's a walk-on part. He's called Garrick.

This evening we went to the nearby village of Duloe. We weren't going to stop at the pub, but I saw a sign outside saying free doggie treats so I dragged the smiley lady in. She thought it only polite to try the local Tribute beer whilst I claimed my free doggy treat.

Day 2
I was bundled into the car and we drove round some winding primrose-

The Secret Adventures of Rolo

filled lanes to a car park and then a strenuous coastal walk around Furze, with its magnificent views of the twinkling sea. The smiley lady was nervous every time I stood near the edge. I did it deliberately.

We descended steeply to the village of Polruan and caught the passenger ferry across to Fowey. The skipper said the fare was 10p per leg for a dog and as I have 4 legs that meant 40p to cross the estuary on his ferry. I folded up a paw and pretended to hop but he didn't fall for it. I liked the boat and the wind whooshing around my whiskers.

The Secret Adventures of Rolo

Fowey — for some unknown reason pronounced Foy, and if you don't say it right they know you are a tourist — is a pretty town to wander around with steep and narrow lanes. The sun shone all day long and, tired out, we retraced our steps back to the Spice Barn (our holiday kennel).

Day 3
We drove to catch the car ferry from Bodinnick to Polkerris. A lovely little beach but no dogs allowed between Easter and September. So we walked along the coastal path to a little beach not quite as far as the village of Par — let's call it Rolo Beach — where I found a big brown dog to play with, fought with the seaweed, explored the rock pools and didn't bark at the sea, nor did I drink

too much seawater.

Day 4

A very short drive to Talland Bay
and we played ball on the beach for
ages. I found a humungous jellyfish
washed up on the beach — it was
bigger than me! It had a kind of
bluish tinge and was quite see-
through. I think it was dead. The
smiley lady kept calling me away
from it.

I clambered over the rocks and
explored the pools and remembered
not to drink the seawater. I was

The Secret Adventures of Rolo

having a lovely time.

Then disaster struck — one of my claws on my back foot got caught on something and started to bleed. It was hanging off. The smiley lady is hopeless at doggy first-aid and a bit squeamish, but luckily there were a couple of friendly builders working nearby who produced some pliers from the toolbox in the back of their van; they took charge and quickly removed the painful claw.

I felt better at once and rewarded the surgeon-builders by licking their faces. They told us that some holidaymakers had lost their dog a couple of days previously when it had escaped from the caravan park where they were staying and that they were keeping their eyes open for it.

I listened to the description of
the dog and knew I'd just seen it
swimming in the bay when I was
investigating the giant jellyfish.
I ran down to the beach woofing,
trying to tell them I'd seen the
lost dog splashing about in the sea
— hard to convey this with woofs —
but they finally understood and one
of the builders set off in his van
to the caravan park to alert the
distraught owners.

I bet the dog had thought to
himself, 'I'm fed up with sitting
around whilst you get yourselves

84

organised. We're here on holiday and I don't want to waste the sunshine. I don't know what you people are up to, but I'm off for a swim!'

Soon swimming dog and anxious owners were reunited. The builders felt as if they were doubling as Animal Rescue on the beach that day. They had also been asked about a missing hawk with a bell on its claw, and yes, they'd seen the bird too. Animal Rescue comes to Talland Bay!

With my paw feeling much better, we set off up the coastal path towards Polperro. This was definitely the steepest uphill walk we've done all week. I was fine, despite the trauma I'd been through; it was the smiley lady who struggled!

85

Polperro is another pretty fishing village and we went into a fish and chip café for lunch.

I sat very patiently under the table whilst the smiley lady declared the fish and chips served in Chips Ahoy were the best she'd tasted anywhere in Cornwall. I was given a bit of batter when she'd finished her meal and then we embarked upon the long cliff walk back to Talland Bay.

A family stopped us en route and asked us if the little dog with the hurty paw was okay. They had witnessed the operation on the beach to remove my broken claw. My fame is spreading!

That night I found a hedgehog in the coal scuttle in the Plough. Not

a real one I hasten to add — a toy
one, with a squeaker. I have never
found a dog toy in a pub before.
Apparently the toy had been
abandoned by a dog visitor at
Christmas. Clever me for finding it.
The landlady said I could keep it.
I used it to wind up the Labrador,
who was very well behaved and
sleeping under the next table, by
squeaking it annoyingly. The smiley
lady stopped smiling and took it off
me until I got back to the cottage.
I slept that night with my paw on
it so it felt loved and safe.

I do enjoy a holiday, but it was
good to get home. I was anxious
in case I'd missed anything on
my patch and straight away ran
upstairs to listen outside the
airing cupboard door, but couldn't
hear anything.

'Rolo, come down at once!' the smiley lady shouted as she carried the bags in from the car. She shut me out in the back garden, so I ran down the steps to tell the rabbits next door that I was back and to blow through the decking at the indestructible toad.

In my absence some blackbirds had built a nest in the hedge, but that's okay — we like garden birds. I only chase wood pigeons. I couldn't wait to tell Athelstan all my news and to hear what was happening in the forest — maybe the bluebells will be out. And I was very pleased that I hadn't missed the hatching!

Chapter 5

Rolo and the Sun Dial

Walking along the footpath beside St George's, the smiley lady spotted a sundial on the church tower and pointed it out to the boy with floppy hair. She remarked that in all the years she had been coming to the church she had never noticed it before.

They looked up at the strange symbols on the clock face and the floppy haired boy already knew that they were Roman numerals but he didn't know how you could possibly tell the time by them.

The smiley lady explained how the sunlight would hit the fixed blade and how that would cast a shadow across the clock face which would in turn point to a number; so you could actually tell the time quite accurately by means of the sun's position in the sky.

'But only on a sunny day,' she added.

'Wait a minute, though,' said the smiley lady, sitting down on a bench to study the old sun dial better, 'the numbers run the opposite way to a normal clock

89

face! It's all back to front. Look it starts with 'I' on the bottom right, and then 'II' and 'III' and 'IV' but wait…there's no 'V'! I wonder why that is? Perhaps it's just worn away.'

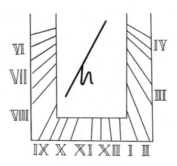

'So what happens at 5 o'clock then?' said the floppy haired boy, screwing his eyes up to peer at the topsy-turvy anti-clockwise face with different sized gaps between the chiselled Roman numerals.

'The rest of the numbers are there, Vl, Vll, Vlll; lX must be nine if it's X for ten 'minus one' and Xl is ten 'plus one' making eleven and Xll, ten 'plus two' for twelve' said the smiley lady.

'What do you make the time, Mum?' he asked, 'I can't make any sense of the time on the sundial can you?'

'Try not to look at the church clock and let's try and work it out,' she said.

'Look at the shadow cast across the clock face and see which number it's pointing to.'

'The shadow is midway between X and Xl so that's about half past ten then,' said the floppy haired boy.

'Well you're almost right,' said the smiley lady.

'The blade has been positioned in the right place to be accurate for Greenwich Mean Time, but you must remember to add an hour to the projected time as we are currently on British Summer Time since we put the clocks forward an hour in March. Obviously you can't alter the time on a sun dial without repositioning it.'

Interesting, I thought, listening to their conversation, and it really concerned me that there was no number five on the sundial. I put it to the back of my mind for now.

The floppy haired boy was telling the smiley lady that he'd read somewhere that when we officially

91

change our clocks from British Summer Time to Greenwich Mean Time putting them back an hour in late October, something really funny happens to Big Ben the most important clock in the country.

'Oh, what's that?' asked the smiley lady, enjoying the conversation with her son.

'They turn off the lights on the clock's four faces because it was thought in the early 20th century, when the action of 'putting the clocks back' first started, that people in London might panic if they glanced up in the night time and saw the big clock's hands going round backwards!'

They both laughed about this and the floppy haired boy said apparently the darkening of the clock continues to this day, despite 21st century people being of much more robust constitution and not so easily scared by time appearing to go into reverse!

'When did they start putting the clocks back then Mum?' he asked.

'I believe it was early in the 1900s,' said the smiley lady, 'we must research it when we get home.'

Later, round the dining room table – with me in hopeful position underneath quietly waiting for spillages – the floppy haired boy read from his lap top that a keen horseman called William Willett thought it was such a 'waste of useful daylight' to be getting up to exercise his horse when the sun was already high in the sky, that he campaigned long and hard from 1907 to have the clocks changed more in line with the sun's rising. But he died in 1915, the year before the government adopted his 'daylight saving' plan. Interestingly, the Germans had also altered their clocks to maximise the daylight hours, and at this time the two countries were of course at war with each other.

The smiley lady added,

'I remember your nan telling me that they tried Double British Summer Time during the Second World War, which meant that clocks were put two hours ahead of Greenwich in the spring, and one hour ahead in winter. She said everybody got terribly confused and the experiment only lasted for the duration of the war. I suppose it might have made 'blackout' easier with shorter night time hours; perhaps that was the rationale behind it.'

I mentioned the upside down sundial to Athelstan that night. I had a feeling he knew something about it and he didn't seem surprised when I told him about the missing digit.

'Have you been there when there is a shadow cast on the space where the five should be?' he asked. Hmmmm. That's what the floppy haired boy had wondered. Food for thought. Speaking of food, I'm hungry. Is it dinner time yet?

Still no activity within the airing cupboard. Hope the egg is all right. Athelstan told me to stop worrying and that it would hatch when it was good and ready and no amount of wishing would hurry along the birth of a dragon.

I spent the next couple of days skulking around the stairs.

I was willing my eyes to bore into the airing cupboard door so I could see through the wood, but I didn't want to draw attention to the makeshift incubator nor its precious contents.

'Mum, Rolo's hanging around the airing cupboard. He's looking guilty like he's wee'd indoors or something.'

I rearranged my indignant facial expression and went downstairs with my tail between my legs.

Dog Blog #5 - According to Rolo

It was time to go to the vet for my annual injection. Now I know most dogs don't like the vets but I see it as a sort of puppy club. Everyone makes a fuss of me and I get weighed and stuff: a tiny injection which I can't even feel, and then I get a biscuit.

Well today's appointment was the first one of the morning and the lady vet was late arriving for work. The smiley lady led me up to the reception desk to check in and

half asleep I put my paws up on the
counter to see what was going on.
Something came up and kissed me on
the nose. I assumed it was a small
dog and was about to go through the
usual routine of doggy greeting but
when I opened my eyes to have a
look who was being over friendly,
to my horror, it was a tabby cat!

The Secret Adventures of Rolo

Now you know I have had close encounters with cats when I time travel, but I have certainly never been kissed by one before… AND I DIDN'T LIKE IT ONE LITTLE BIT!

The cat turned its back on me and started licking its paws without a care in the world. The receptionist was laughing and said,

'Oh, don't mind George, he deliberately winds the dogs up.'
I was mortified. I was skating on the lino with my claws when the smiley lady took a firm grip of my lead; she then sandwiched my wriggling body between her knees. I was making baby seal noises. Let me at it, I'd soon wipe the smirk off it's silly round face!

This pantomime went on for about

10 minutes and at last the vet
appeared and when she listened
to my heart rate she said it was
beating rather faster than was
normal for a small dog. The smiley
lady snorted and said it was 'not
surprising as you're late and he's
just been kissed by a cat in your
waiting room!'

Great. Now everyone knows about it.
We will have to go to a different
vet in future. My reputation is at
stake. ☹

Chapter 6

Rolo and Magna Carta

'Do you remember King John?' said Athelstan the next night.

How could I forget the grumpy English king who, when he came to grant the people of Marlborough a Royal Charter back in 1204, had ignored my request for a permanent doggy bowl in the High Street? Although to be fair, he did take on board my suggestion of a twice weekly market in the town.

I put my head on one side to show I was listening, and dropped the pink ball.

'We need your tactful negotiating skills again,' said Athelstan.

'You'll see why when you get there…good luck…off you go,' and, with that, I found myself staring at the oak tree with the time tunnel yawning ahead of me, and Yulia and Da impatiently waving their lanterns in the entrance.

99

Yulia explained that after our last meeting in the 13th century, King John had gone around the country appeasing his subjects by dishing out royal charters in return for support from his people.

However, his goodwill was short-lived and he had once again overstepped the mark by forcing extremely heavy taxation on the barons, called 'scutage'; the money raised by this taxation he used to pay mercenaries to go and fight his battles. It seems that English barons were not too keen to embark on costly campaigns abroad as they rarely had their expenses reimbursed by the King.

King John had also introduced something called 'amercement', which was a hefty fine on people for neglect of public duty. This law was a bit vague. If you 'offended against the King's peace' you could be fined for pretty much doing or not doing anything. The ruling was deliberately woolly and could not be argued against, so the barons were getting pretty annoyed. It seemed King John had not learned his lessons from their last confrontation. He was corrupting the justice system to blackmail his barons and gain money for the Crown. King John was not going to win any popularity contest in 1215.

The time tunnel led me to the centre of a big yew tree with a hole in its trunk. We were in a place called Ankerwycke in the grounds of a small priory.

Well, I certainly wouldn't forget where the entrance was this time! I glanced back into the tree. Yulia and Da had already disappeared with their lanterns, into the safety of the tunnel.

A lady wearing a tall pointy hat draped with a veil glided towards me. I say 'glided' because she moved so serenely it seemed that she was on wheels.

She bent down to pat me and I imagined her voice to be soft and gentle and tinkling like a tiny bell.

I asked her where King John could be found and her lovely face darkened a little. She didn't seem to be surprised to be spoken to by a dog. She wouldn't speak to me, however, but pointed through the woodland, to a gate on the other side of the priory gardens. I pricked up an ear and heard the very distant but unmistakable sound of angry men.

Hmmm, that rumble of discontent was in deep contrast to the peace and tranquillity within the grounds of the priory, but there was nothing else for it: I was on a mission and ran off in the direction of the noise.

It seemed I had arrived at a makeshift royal court. Looking about I spied a large fancy tent – the source of the commotion.

All manner of people were raising their voices, trying to make their demands heard. The sound under the awning was deafening. I followed the general direction of their anger and recognised at once the unmistakable figure of King John: a surly man with unkempt black hair, scowling as he slumped in an ornamental seat. His crown was wedged down on his head trying to tame his locks. I thought it best to keep out of his way and hid under the table, just out of range of his outstretched legs, trying hard to make sense of what was going on.

A familiar voice cleared the tent; it was the scribe whom I'd encountered during a previous time travelling adventure.

The Secret Adventures of Rolo

He must have been promoted since our last meeting.
The man had grown in stature and his voice
carried authority' but he sounded rather weary
as he entreated the barons to go and take lunch
and promised that they would reconvene their
discussions in the afternoon.

I'm sure I was the only one to notice from beneath
the table that he had his fingers crossed behind his
back.

The King stood up in a rage and knocked his chair
over, flinging the golden crown across the table.
He stormed off in the opposite direction to the
disgruntled barons. The scribe righted the chair with
a sigh and placed the crown on the table next to the
document.

I poked my head out from underneath the table
covering.

'Oh, it's you again! Got any bright ideas about how
to get the barons off the King's back this time have
you, scruffy?' The scribe bent down and roughly
stroked my ears.

I imagined that it had been a difficult morning. I submitted to his ruffling, and then asked if I could see what had been agreed already.

I climbed upon the great ornamental chair still warm from the royal posterior, and put my paws on the table making an important stance, pretending for a moment that I was the king. The scribe put the crown on my head, but it was a bit big and slipped over one ear.

The hapless scribe pushed the document towards me jabbing his finger at the relevant bits. He explained that if they did not reach some agreement that day, then the whole of England would fall into the hands of the French. The barons, fed up with broken promises, had already started negotiating with the French crown prince and the prospect of England being ruled by the French was becoming more and more likely.

I scanned the document, pleased to find that I could read Medieval Latin. There was a lot of stuff about feudal payments and regulations concerning inheritance for widows and children, and waffle

The Secret Adventures of Rolo

about money and other economic matters.

A very important point was that the sale of justice would be forbidden – this was after all bribery – and the unpopular taxations of 'scutage' and 'amercement' should cease immediately. Furthermore, debts and tariffs should be regulated and most importantly it would not be possible to imprison a free man without trial by his peers. Foreigners could no longer be appointed to important positions over English barons and indeed all foreign knights and mercenaries should return at once to whence they came.

Now I might only be a small dog, but even I realised the importance of such a document. I knew, with the wisdom of foresight, that it would go on to become the backbone of law in England and have further significance in the world, albeit with quite a lot of revisions over the next few years.

The part of the charter that the King really didn't like was the 'security clause', which gave twenty-five barons permission to force the King to sign for the 'community of the realm' or else face imprisonment.

This was serious stuff, giving the barons ultimate power over the King. Reading on, I could see nothing in there about my requested doggy bowls. I would have to do something about that.

The scribe went off to find himself some lunch, muttering and shaking his head, knowing that this was not going to be a peaceful agreement as the King was in no mood to give up any of his assumed power. He didn't ask me if I wanted anything to eat.

I saw the abandoned quill lying on the table and seized my chance. I first glanced around to make sure no one was looking, then I snatched it up and dipped it in the ink.

The Secret Adventures of Rolo

I started to write in my neatest script, copying the style of the letters: 'canine…'.

'What do you think you're doing to the Great Charter?' bellowed King John, as he snatched the precious document away from me in mid-sentence, smudging the words I had written with his sleeve.

I jumped down and hid once more in the folds of the tablecloth, hopefully out of sight, and trying to stop shaking with fear. The crown rolled onto the floor.

I had missed an opportunity here and once more it seemed my simple request would go un-granted. The King sat for an hour or so, with his head in his hands, gnashing his teeth and complaining loudly about the injustice of the demands that his royal personage would have to give up.

When the scribe returned to the negotiating table, followed closely by the rebellious barons, the mood had changed – amazing what effect lunch can have in a crisis – and proceedings recommenced slightly more smoothly.

The spokesman for the barons explained that King John had no choice: concede or give up the throne and the kingdom of England to France. The scribe nervously pushed the ink pot towards the angry king, not daring to look up nor make eye contact with the disempowered monarch.

He felt around desperately for his abandoned writing implement, but it was nowhere to be seen.

The scribe lifted the cloth, peered under the table and scowled at me. I was still doing my terrier shake. Luckily he didn't notice my guilty secret.

In the surprise of being discovered red-pawed amending the charter, I had taken the quill to my hiding place and in my panic I had snapped it clean in half with my teeth. The scribe feared that a further delay whilst a fresh quill was brought might cause King John to retract his already wavering consent.

Instead, the scribe roared for sealing wax and much to the King's surprise he grabbed the royal hand and thrust the signet ring into the hot red liquid and

The Secret Adventures of Rolo

pushed it down, dripping onto the document, thus affixing the royal seal to Magna Carta. The King was amazed by the audacity of the scribe, but knew he was cornered and had no choice. What use was a king without a kingdom?

The Great Charter had been sealed and that was good enough to send the barons home muttering amongst themselves, although some would still have liked to have imprisoned the King as threatened.

And so you see, Magna Carta, which, after numerous revisions, went on to become the basis of the English justice system and the model of the United States Bill of Rights in 1791, as well as the foundation of the Universal Declaration of Human Rights in 1948, was not actually signed in ink by the belligerent king as is often depicted in historic paintings.

No, it was not signed because a little Jack Russell ran off with the quill whilst trying to add his own clause – or should that be 'claws' – about statutory dog bowls.

I ran back through the woodland to the priory and luckily the gate was still open. I saw the silhouette of the prioress within and I circled the yew tree, looking for the hole that would lead me to the time tunnel. I was very relieved to see a familiar glow of lanterns and dived headlong into the hole.

On the way back, I told Yulia all that had happened and I asked her why the prioress wouldn't speak to me.

'She had probably taken a 'vow of silence', the woodland girl answered quite simply. I hadn't thought of that. I wasn't used to humans ever being silent!

The next night when it was dark and everyone was in bed including me, I heard furious tapping on the kitchen window and knew that only meant one thing: Athelstan had sent Yulia and Bubo the owl to summon me for another important task. I wondered where we were off to this time, and remembered to take the pink ball with me. I dropped it at the base of the Athelstan tree as I wagged my tail in greeting.

'So you nearly scuppered the signing of Magna Carta did you Little Pup?' roared Athelstan, but I could sense by his tone, despite the darkness, that he was smiling.

'What happened after the signing – erm - sealing of the charter then Athelstan, did the barons go back to their castles and the King start behaving better towards his subjects?' I asked, curious to know the outcome of the story.

'Not exactly,' said Athelstan and he went on to explain that the bullying continued and the following year French Prince Louis invaded the South East of England and King John retreated leaving the French ruling a third of England,

including London, with full baronial support –
unheard of in the whole of English history!

'The pope declared the charter unlawful. Just a year
after the historic charter was – harrumph – 'sealed',
fugitive King John died of dysentery leaving his
young son to rule as Henry lll and it was left to
others to drive the French from English shores. It
took two more kings and various revisions of Magna
Carta to make it into the law we still adhere to today.
To sum up, everyone, even the king or queen of
England, is subject to the law,' he finished his speech
with a flourish.

So now you know.

Dog blog #6 - According to Rolo

The smiley lady had been to yoga
and was hungry and needed comfort
food. I watched her get the milk
bottle out from the fridge door
and mix a little with some custard
powder and sugar. She poured the
rest of the milk into a saucepan

The Secret Adventures of Rolo

to bring it carefully to the boil. She then mixed in the yellow stuff and when it had thickened she carefully poured herself a big bowl of homemade custard over a sliced banana. She set it on the dining room table to cool down and went upstairs to get changed as it was piping hot: so hot the steam was rising off it.

I quickly glanced around the table and saw a chair left slightly out. In a trice I was up on that table and had gulped down the steaming custard and sliced bananas leaving the bowl completely clean, even under the spoon.

113

'Rolo, what are you up to?' I heard her coming back downstairs and was afraid she'd heard the tell-tale clanking of my tag on the side of the bowl — usually my sign to let her know my water bowl is empty.

I was already lying meekly in my basket licking my lips to get rid of the delicious but incriminating custard. From the corner of my half closed eyes I could see her lifting the spoon and inspecting the bowl and then going back to the hob to see if she had actually poured the custard from the saucepan or if she had just thought she had.

When the smiley lady put two and two together, she said I could forget any thoughts of supper. I was pretty full anyway. I heard her explaining to the floppy haired boy

when he came home from school, and
both tried to hide their laughter
as they were pretending to be cross
with me.

Chapter 7

Rolo and the Knight's Effigy

As coincidence would have it, the floppy haired boy was full of talk of Magna Carta when he came home from school.

Because it was the 'octocentenary' (I may have made that word up, but, hey listen, it's not bad for a dog – I mean eight hundredth anniversary) of the signing … erm … sealing, children all over the country have been studying the famous document at school.

The smiley lady was looking in a telephone book as she half listened to the floppy haired boy.

'Sorry, love, what was that? Yes I am listening, it's just that there are some strange noises coming from the water tank in the airing cupboard and I really need a plumber to investigate what's going on pretty sharpish before the temperature drops and we shall need the heating on every day. Now, what were you saying?'

I froze, rooted to the spot, with an ear up, wondering

how I could get to the airing cupboard undetected, and as quickly as possible.

'So, mum, we're going to Salisbury Cathedral to see a real version of Magna Carta in an exhibition there,' the floppy haired boy said excitedly, waving a permission letter at the smiley lady. 'There are only four copies in the whole of England!'

'Shame you can't come with me – it would be really cool!' he said to me. I flipped over on my back for a tummy rub, wishing I could communicate with him like I can other humans when I time travel. My mind was preoccupied with the strange noise in the airing cupboard.

'Mum, quick…look, Rolo's got a funny expression on his face!'

Eventually, the smiley lady left the house with a rolled yoga mat under her arm and the floppy haired boy went out on his skateboard, so at last I had the house to myself.

I hoovered the kitchen floor for crumbs and then raced up the stairs two at a time and flung the airing cupboard door wide open.

Two beady eyes glared at me from within the pile of tea towels and I heard a strange squawking sound. The egg had hatched!

I poked my head into the nest of towels and was rewarded by a nip on my inquisitive nose. Now what was I going to do? It was one thing to hide an immobile egg indoors and quite another to conceal a baby dragon! I had to find a new hiding place pretty quick because I'd seen a note beside the phone to say the plumber was coming tomorrow. Think, Rolo, think!

With no time to lose, I gathered up the four corners

of the tea towel and carried the squirming bundle downstairs and into the kitchen.

This time I did drop it in the bucket whilst I struggled to open the trapdoor and then I dragged the bucket by carrying its handle in my mouth to the back garage door.

Luckily the door wasn't locked, and, using the stool the smiley lady uses to rest the washing basket on, I managed to open the door by leaning heavily on the handle. I left the bucket outside whilst I entered the gloom of the garage.

I looked about, searching for a safe haven, desperately trying to think what to do next with my charge. I spied an old cupboard, no longer useful in the house and kept in storage for goodness knows what purpose.

Surely no one would be looking in there! I found some empty sacks and some earthy compost and old curtains used to cover the furniture when the interior of the house was being decorated. I set to work making a temporary dragon shelter and then thought that perhaps the hatchling was hungry and that's why it was making a funny noise from within the bucket.

For now, though, I went back out into the garden and found the tray of a flower pot that had collected rainwater and I tipped the tiny dragon out so he could have a drink. When he had had his fill he started hopping about the rotary washing line which gave me the chance to have a better look at him.

I assumed it was a 'him'. He kept cheeping at me and trying to follow me, waddling like a duckling and waggling his newly hatched wings which didn't quite open yet and resembled a folded umbrella. I was surprised to see that he was pale in colour, white in fact. I expected him to be red like Rhydian.

I eventually coaxed him back into the bucket, then carried it again by the handle into the open garage. I tipped the dragon into the cupboard and shut the door quickly.

'I'll be back with food later,' I said and ran back in the house. Scanning the kitchen there was no food to be seen. I'd have to share my dinner – that's unheard of!

Later that evening, when the people were back indoors, the doorbell ringing set me off barking and the smiley lady tucked me under her arm as she opened the door to admit the plumber. She shut me in the kitchen and escorted him upstairs to show him the airing cupboard.

When he came back down about twenty minutes later, he came into the kitchen, scratched his head and then removed a pencil stub from behind his ear and proceeded to write a bill for the call out charge.

'I've tightened all the joints and tested the pipes and the boiler seems to be working fine. You've plenty of hot water. I would say something has been nesting in there by the looks of things, though I couldn't find any mouse droppings, just a few bits of what looks like plaster from the walls. I've cleared the mess up. That'll be fifty pounds, please. Don't hesitate to ring if you hear any more strange sounds, but I think it's all fixed.'

Fifty pounds! That seemed a bit excessive and he can't have actually done anything other than use a dustpan and brush!

I felt a bit guilty and slunk off to my basket.

When it was tea time, I wolfed my food down and uncharacteristically ran manically around the kitchen with my mouth full.

'Rolo, eat more slowly, you'll get indigestion,' scolded the smiley lady.

I started scrabbling at the back door.

'Oh, you want to go out do you? Off you go, then. That'll teach you for gobbling your food!'

The Secret Adventures of Rolo

My mouth was bulging with doggy biscuits. I dropped them in a heap on the path whilst I struggled with the garage door. I picked up the biscuits again and deposited them at the feet of the hungry hatchling. I let him hop around the garage for a bit and then had to shush him back into his little hiding place. He really didn't want to go.

'I'll be back as soon as I can,' I whispered and scurried back to the patio door and woofed to let them know to let me back in. We all watched television for a while. I kept an ear up.

As soon as the occupants of the house went to bed, I wasted no time in rushing to Athelstan to tell him that the egg had hatched.

'The hatchling can't stay in the garage; he's making too much noise!' I garbled, anxious to sort out the problem.

'Don't worry, little pup, you can bring him back to the forest very soon. Yulia and Da have been busy searching for a place for him to grow up safely, where we can all keep an eye on him. I'll send word

123

when we are ready for him. For now you must keep him as quiet as you can.'

Over the next few days, I had to be very devious in taking things from the kitchen to feed the hungry hatchling…crusts of toast, an unopened packet of biscuits from the larder (luckily not in a tin) and more of my doggy biscuits smuggled outside. I even fought a magpie for a suet ball that he'd stolen from the bird table thinking hatchlings can probably eat anything! I was running out of ideas, though, and hoped Yulia would come for us soon.

One evening, I heard a tapping on the back door. I must have left the garage door open and the cupboard door ajar! I barked to be let out and quickly rounded him up, thankful that no one else had heard him.

Imagine the floppy haired boy's surprise if he discovered he had a baby dragon in his garage!

When he returned from his school trip to Salisbury, the floppy haired boy was very excited about all the knights' tombs he had seen along the aisles of the famous cathedral, the construction of which had started in 1220, just five years after the 'sealing' of Magna Carta.

'Do you know what, mum?' he told the smiley lady, talking to her from his perch on a kitchen stool whilst she cooked his favourite dinner, shepherd's pie.

'What's that, love?' she asked, alternately stirring the mince and mashing the potatoes in a frenzy of activity. (I hope she saves me some minced meat and I bet the hatchling would like some too.)

'Something odd I discovered in Salisbury Cathedral today. All of the medieval knights' tombs have something carved at their feet, whether it's an animal or a mythical beast from their family crest. All of them that is, except one!'

'Really?' said the smiley lady absentmindedly as she tasted the mince for seasoning, 'I wonder why that might be?'

Well even if SHE wasn't that interested, I certainly was. I raised an ear to listen better, while the floppy

125

haired boy continued sharing what he'd learned.

A little while later, I managed to sneak some leftover shepherd's pie out to the hatchling in the garage and still he kept cheeping at me like a newly hatched chick.

'I doubt you can understand me, but it's really important that you keep quiet!' I implored, as I shut him back in the cupboard.

I went to find Athelstan and told him that the rehoming matter was becoming more urgent, and he said only one more day was required and the new home for the hatchling would be ready. I was relieved and assured him he was secure for the night.

Then I told him what the floppy haired boy had said about the tomb of the knight without a mascot in Salisbury Cathedral.

'You had better go and find out about the knight then, Little Pup! You sound as if you are in need of adventure. Go on, back to the 13th century with you. Have you got the orb?'

The Secret Adventures of Rolo

Luckily I had brought the pink ball 'just in case' and I dropped it and moved forwards towards the hole in the base of the tree. Yulia and Da were already there with their lanterns. I had no idea what I might be getting into this time.

I seemed to be back at court, but not that of the unpopular King John. His successor was a boy called Henry.

I decided the best course of action, like on my last visit, was to stay hidden and see what unfolded.

I found my favourite hiding place underneath a long trestle table and watched a boy, seated high up on the dais, presuming this to be the young king. I hoped fervently that the feasting knights were messy eaters for I was suddenly extremely hungry and there was a delicious aroma of roasting meat lingering in the air.

Beneath the table I found myself nestled in between a pair of large feet and, to my immense surprise, a bone was passed down by a big hand and held out for me to take. I took it gratefully, remembering my

The Secret Adventures of Rolo

manners and not snatching.

A few other bits of meat followed and then a bowl of water was handed down and placed carefully on the floor.

I looked up into the kind eyes of a man with black curly hair, and thought he looked a bit familiar. The kindly man smiled, belched and then bent down and wiped his greasy hands on me. Now steady on! That's what greyhounds are for, not me! I am not a canine serviette! But I remained silent and put up with the rough handling, licking the grease off with great indignation and a look of disdain.

When he had finished eating, the knight got to his feet and scooped me up and tucked me under his arm. I was lifted a very long way off the ground for he was a very tall man indeed.

'God speed, Uncle William! What have you got there? A puppy for me?' called the young boy from the dais and I buried my face in the knight's cloak in case he felt obliged to hand me over, but I needn't have worried.

The Secret Adventures of Rolo

'Good night, my liege,' replied the knight, bowing low to his king and nearly dropping me on the floor, but carefully concealing me with this movement underneath his cloak.

Suddenly I realised whom the tall knight reminded me of; this was King John's half-brother, William Longespee, Earl of Salisbury and Sheriff of Wiltshire (amongst other high offices).

'You shall be my faithful hound; I need a mascot; I'm not giving you up to become the young king's pet!'

William Longespee lifted me high in the air with his hand supporting my tummy and then patted me on the rump as he laid me across the pommel of his saddle before climbing astride his big horse.

The horse eyed me suspiciously. I gulped. I remembered what happened to faithful hounds and wasn't sure I wanted to be one. I was thinking back to my encounter with Prince Llewellyn in a previous adventure. Not much I could do right now as I lay sprawled across this huge horse and held with a firm hand.

The Secret Adventures of Rolo

We galloped off at great speed and the tall knight made it clear he wanted me to become his companion and ride into battle with him, as a lucky mascot against the French or anyone else who might invade. I wasn't sure about any of this.

He took me to Salisbury Cathedral. It was even more impressive in the thirteenth century than it is today because there was not much around it. The beautiful cathedral completely dominated its landscape with nothing to detract from its magnificence.

'I was here in 1220 when the foundation stone was laid,' the knight explained to me as he carried me around the interior to the East End.

'This is the plot I have earmarked for my tomb when my time comes and, look, here is the elaborate wooden chest which will hold my bones, and see the great likeness the sculptor is working on now, carving out from stone a perpetual memory of me. I will be painted in the family colours of blue and gold with lions on my shield. I'm so excited, it's all ready for me, but the one thing missing from this happy scene is YOU!'

I had no idea what this knight was talking about, and then I realised what he intended. It seemed that animals didn't like him. Whether it was because he was so big and scary, or for whatever reason, every dog he'd ever owned had run away. He wanted the sculptor to copy my likeness so that when HIS time for eternal rest came – God willing quite a few years hence – the great knight would be depicted with his feet on the unusual little dog he had rescued and was now parading around like some kind of status symbol.

I heard Longespee telling the sculptor that he would bring his little dog tomorrow to sit for a study, so that the likeness could be created in position at the feet of the knight for the tomb. I was in two minds about that news. Much as I wanted to make my mark on history and be famous forever, I wasn't sure that I wanted to be commemorated in stone as a medieval knight's foot rest!

Anyway I had to get back to my basket and I was worried about outstaying my visit. I had to find an excuse to get away from the tall knight and this was proving difficult because he insisted on carrying me everywhere, as if I was too precious to use my paws!

He even talked of dressing me up in a velvet cloak, and making me a suit of armour. Not cool. I could imagine Chickpea and the other dogs laughing at me all dressed up like a doll.

Out of the corner of my eye I saw a rat scurry across the nave and I seized my chance. I leapt out from the tall knight's arms. It was a long way to the stone floor but thankfully I landed on my feet.

Longespee called anxiously after me in a shrill voice, but I was on a mission. When the knight caught sight of what I was chasing, he screamed in a most un-knightly fashion – it would appear the brave earl with the famously long sword was terrified of rodents!

I chased the rat up the aisle, through the tall and narrow nave with its grey stone walls and dark polished Purbeck marble columns. We were almost at the high altar.

I spied the rat cowering behind a column.

'Psssst! You can go now,' I whispered to the quivering rodent. 'Go on, scarper! Vamoose!'

I waved my paws shooing the rat away, but it seemed petrified with fear. This was no good; I needed it to disappear! I didn't want to have to actually catch the thing – it was merely the agent of my escape.

'Go!' I hissed again and turned away giving it the chance to scurry off into the sanctuary of the altar cloth.

I seized my chance and crept down the shadowy steps to the crypt with the sound of William Longespee's squeals still ringing in my ears. 'Come back, come back little doggy, I need you; we will make a fabulous team…'

If I didn't get out from here fast I'd be trapped in the 13th century forever with this crazy knight who couldn't keep a pet! No wonder all the others had all run away! I had no idea how to get back to the time tunnel as the entrance was some distance away but suddenly I spied a tiny light coming from behind one of the tombs. It looked like someone was trying to attract my attention as the light flickered like some kind of code.

Yulia!

'I thought I'd come and see what you're up to as you have been missing quite a while. I've found another entrance to the time tunnel here in the crypt. Let's go!' cried the tiny lamp bearer pleased to have come to my rescue.

I fervently wished I could explain to the floppy haired boy the answer to his question as to why the stone effigy of William Longespee was the only knight in the cathedral not to have an animal to rest his feet on, but alas I'll have to keep that knowledge to myself.

I did wonder what happened to the hapless knight and Athelstan allowed me to satisfy my curiosity by sending me back to Salisbury Cathedral nearly 600 years later, in 1791 to be precise. Isn't that the beauty of time travel? I also wanted to know what happened to the cathedral rat that had unwittingly aided my escape after I had allowed him to get away.

'The answer is in his tomb,' called Athelstan into the time tunnel, his words hanging eerily in the air as I followed the bobbing lanterns through the tunnel.

18th century Salisbury was very different to my previous visit. Lots of impressive houses had been built in an area called The Close and there were formal gardens laid out with shrubberies and exotic plants introduced by aristocratic gentlemen who had completed The Grand Tour – which was the equivalent of a modern day gap year – and who had brought back souvenirs, in this case plants. The cathedral itself was just as impressive; this was after all the tallest church spire in England.

Rumour had it that William Longespee had been poisoned in 1226 – as it happened, not so very long after my visit. It was lucky that he had already designed his own tomb, I thought.

I had to get someone to open the tomb; that was what Athelstan had implied.

I peered through an open door and saw a clerk to the justices and, from his nondescript appearance, I considered he could do with something to help make his name; something dynamic to get himself noticed in the legal world.

As luck would have it, he could understand me, and didn't seem too surprised to be having a discussion with a small but well-mannered, intelligent dog.

He listened to what I had to say, and got up from his desk, carefully placing the quill next to the ink well. Perhaps he had heard that I snapped them in a previous century!

We were in a room stuffed from floor to ceiling with books, and he climbed a ladder to reach an ancient tome from its lofty shelf, bringing down a great deal of dust with it. He blew a cloud of dust off the cover and thumbed through the pages of the weighty volume and then read aloud,

'According to Roger of Wendover who commentated on court events during that time, Longespee was thought to have been poisoned by a man called Hubert de Burgh, but for some reason de Burgh was never brought to trial. That's very strange as Longespee was loyal to King Henry lll, so I wonder why justice was not prescribed?'

'Perhaps his tomb might hold some clues?' I threw in as casually as I could.

'Well, if we are going to examine whatever remains of the knight, we need to do it under cover of darkness which means sneaking into the cathedral. They have been demolishing the Hungerford Chantry on the north side of the Trinity Chapel and the tombs are being relocated, which should make our investigation a little easier. I was in the cathedral only yesterday and noticed that they were in the process of moving them so let's hope we can find Longspee without too much problem.'

We passed the time until darkness fell and, after a shared supper of bread and meat, we set off.

The tremendous wooden cathedral door opened with a loud creak and unobserved we entered the nave.

It was very dark inside the cathedral, and every sound echoed. I tried not to skitter on the flagstones.

'Over here, it's the painted one,' I called, and the clerk must have wondered how on earth I knew in the darkness exactly which tomb belonged to the former Earl of Salisbury.

'It's a long story,' I said, pre-empting his question, 'but trust me, this is him, the one without a dog at his feet.'

The workmen who were moving the tombs had made our task a lot easier. They had already shifted the heavy stone effigy. I told the clerk I would stand guard whilst he lifted the lid of the wooden box which was the tomb containing the remains of the medieval knight.

You will not believe what we found when we exhumed the remains of William Longespee!

Delicate readers, pray skip the next sentence.

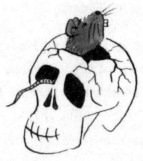

A black rat, still (as was later found) with traces of arsenic in its body, lay perfectly preserved inside the knight's skull, thus proving the poisoning theory, even if it didn't confirm who had actually administered the poison.

'I wonder why he is the only knight without his feet on a trusty companion, especially with him being the first person to have been interred inside the cathedral?' said the clerk, running his hands over the stone effigy which had been moved to stand beside the wooden tomb. He was already thinking about the impact the discovery might have on advancing his career and was wrapping up the rat in his handkerchief to take back to his office as evidence.

'Perhaps he just didn't like animals?' I added casually, smiling in the dark.

I was anxious to get back to my basket now my curiosity had been satisfied. It had been a busy couple of nights with all this century-hopping back and forth to Salisbury, and lack of sleep was catching up with me. I took my leave of the 18th century and at last fell exhausted into bed, snuggling into my blankets, hoping against hope that it was a long time until morning.

Chapter 8

The Dragon Rehomed

The next night I was summoned to the kitchen window by an urgent tapping. It was Yulia and Bubo the owl and they said it was time to bring the hatchling to Athelstan.

Hurrah, I thought, not rating the nursery maid job too highly.

Yulia waited patiently in the back garden whilst I climbed through the trapdoor. Luckily the pram was still on the decking. Bubo perched on the handle to steady it and Yulia helped me fetch the baby dragon from the cupboard in the garage and bundle him into the pram. I had to put a sack over him to stop the flapping and squawking and all the while Yulia was speaking a strange language in soothing tones.

We must have been quite a funny sight: a small dog, an owl, a woodland girl, and a doll's pram containing a squirming squawking sack with a head poking out, as we made our way to the sanctuary of the forest.

Athelstan bent down to examine the hatchling and announced very grandly that his name was to be Gwyn, explaining that Gwyn meant 'white' in Welsh. The white dragon! The penny dropped.

'Take him to his new home,' Athelstan said, and Yulia and I wheeled Gwyn in his chariot to the edge of the forest.

Bubo flew on ahead, leading the way. Yulia explained to me that there had once been an old quarry on the edge of the forest which had long fallen into disuse. She and Bubo had found the perfect hiding place where Gwyn could live and grow strong: the hatchling's new home would be a concealed cave.

142

The Secret Adventures of Rolo

We pressed on through overgrown brambles to a much lesser known part of the forest and I spied a rocky outcrop through the bushes.

'We'll have to leave the pram here and continue on foot.'

'I think it best to keep Gwyn in the sack for now in case he hops away,' said Yulia, and again she spoke to the bewildered dragon with soothing words.

Between us we managed to drag the sack the last few hundred yards through the brambles to the mouth of a cave.

'Wait! I've forgotten something!' Yulia went back to the abandoned pram and, rummaging around, produced her lantern.

We entered the cave following the light of the tiny lantern, which made the shadows seem very large and scary as they danced on the stone walls.

'Can we let Gwyn out now?' I asked, concerned for his wellbeing.

'Just a little bit further inside,' said Yulia, and Bubo hopped on ahead leading the way to a smaller cave which would serve very well as a hiding place for the hatchling.

Eventually the owl and woodland girl were satisfied, and we put the sack down on the floor. At once an angry head popped out, but when it saw me it started squeaking more with affection than anger.

'Gwyn thinks you're his parent!' laughed Yulia. She opened up the sack and the tiny dragon hopped out and started looking around at his surroundings. Bubo left us in the cave and I wondered what he was up to. Presently he came back with twigs in his mouth. He made this journey about twenty times, never once pausing to rest until his work was done.

The Secret Adventures of Rolo

Yulia instructed me to gather the sticks and to try
to find moss or something to soften the dragon's
bed. I followed Bubo to the entrance of the cave,
borrowing Yulia's tiny lantern, and then set about
scraping moss off the stones and carrying it back
to our makeshift dragon's den. The three of us
worked hard, trying to make Gwyn's new home as
comfortable as possible.

When Yulia was satisfied with her nest building, she
patted the moss covered pile of sticks and Gwyn
hopped on it and settled down.

'We'll be back with some food. Be sure to stay in the
cave,' she warned, as we took our leave and headed
back through the forest to our own homes.

145

The Secret Adventures of Rolo

I would love to have been a fly on the wall in that cave and could imagine Gwyn inquisitively exploring his new home, sticking his dragon snout into every nook and cranny. I just hoped he heeded Yulia's warning to stay well hidden.

Chapter 9

Rolo and Henry Vlll

I wished I could share my secret with the floppy haired boy. Imagine his face if I could take him into the forest and show him the baby dragon in the cave!

I was truly tempted to share my secret, but the trouble was I knew jolly well he would not be able to keep the secret to himself. Even if he did not tell the smiley lady, he would be bound to tell someone at school and even if he swore them to secrecy, news would spread like a forest fire because of the very nature of the thing, and Gwyn's life would surely be endangered. I could not take that risk.

Yulia and Da kept Gwyn fed with wild rabbits from the warren, and I shared my doggy biscuits every now and then.

The little dragon grew stronger and stronger and was soon testing his wings in the cave and before long Yulia said he would want to fly. Uh-oh. That sounded like fun and danger all at the same time. It would be some time before the hatchling was strong

147

enough to carry me on his back as Rhydian had done.

It seemed ages since I'd had a time travelling adventure because my nights were taken up with looking after my charge, but then Athelstan summoned me and said he wanted me to go back to St Mary's Priory at Ankerwycke.

'Did I miss something in the 13th century?' I asked, hoping I was not going to have to see King John again.

'No, this is a different king and a different problem; off you go Little Pup!' said the tree dragon. I dropped the pink ball among the tree roots and looked about for my light bearer.

Yulia escorted me through the time tunnel as Da was on dragon duty that night and we chatted about Gwyn and I asked the woodland girl when she thought the dragon would be ready to fly.

'I don't think it will be long,' she said, and, anxious to get back to help Da with Gwyn, she turned on her heel and left me once more in the middle of the old yew tree.

I recognised the place at once, mainly by the smell of the yew resin, but what surprised me was that the girth of the tree had increased a lot since my last visit and it took a while to find my way out from the middle of the tree.

It wasn't only the tree which had expanded: the priory had grown a little in size too and now had a small building extension attached to it. I hoped that this was a sign that the small community was prospering.

There were half a dozen nuns tending the neatly

planted rows of vegetables with hoes and garden forks. The prioress was overseeing their work and she rolled her sleeves up and joined in. She was dressed in a similar style to the other prioress but her wimple was different. Thinking about it, I don't suppose church fashion changes that much down the centuries.

There were cows and sheep enclosed in a small field; very likely the priory was self-sufficient, producing enough food to feed the sisters.

I glanced around, as I hadn't yet worked out which king I would be meeting in this place or even which year it was. There were no obvious clues.

Uh-oh, the prioress has seen me and was heading over…

'Aw, petit chien, come, are you hungry? Do you need a drink?' The lady came towards me with outstretched hands and I thought I could be on to a good thing here.

She knelt down on the path and fondled my ears. I obliged by rolling over for a tummy rub. At least this

150

The Secret Adventures of Rolo

prioress didn't seem to have taken a vow of silence. I noticed at once that everyone spoke French around here. Was it the fashion or had we been invaded? I wondered.

'Quel est votre nom?' she asked. Now my French isn't that brilliant – I had learned a smattering from the floppy haired boy, which I used during my Montgolfier balloon flight – but I guessed she was asking my name.

'Je m'appelle Rolo,' I answered shyly and her face lit up with a sweet smile.

'Et je m'appelle Alice,' she answered, shaking my paw. 'Je suis heureux de faire votre connaissance.'

Pleased to meet you too, nice lady, but my limited French vocabulary had run out.

'Viens ici, Rolo, vite, regardez!'

What did she want me to see, I wondered.

I followed her and she crouched behind a wall in the vegetable garden putting her forefinger to her lips to

151

shush me.

A tall but stocky man with reddish hair appeared, wearing very ornate clothing. It surprised me that he was alone, as he had a regal air about him and was surely a royal personage!

The man stood under the straggly boughs of the great tree and I could hear him humming a tune to himself. It sounded like 'Greensleeves'. He was obviously waiting for someone.

The prioress smiled at me and returned her gaze to the king.

A few moments later we could hear giggling, and a few pretty ladies dressed in fine clothes and jewels appeared, fussing around a striking lady with a very important air about her. She wore a necklace with the letter 'B' hanging around her slender neck.

'Who are these people?' I whispered to the prioress and she bent down to reply

'Why, it's Henry Vlll and the lady is Anne Boleyn. They often meet here when the king is in the area.

The Secret Adventures of Rolo

They sit a while and talk. She giggles a lot. Her ladies-in-waiting go into the priory to take tea to give them privacy.'

Ah, so that's what the phrase 'lady-in-waiting' means then, I thought to myself: hanging around making yourself invisible until you are needed.

'Divorced, beheaded, died; divorced, beheaded, survived' I muttered under my breath, remembering the rhyme recited by the floppy haired boy about the fate of Henry Vlll's wives.

'Excusez-moi, petit chien?' the lovely prioress asked what I was saying.

'Erm nothing… Are they married?'

'Oh la la, mais non!' the prioress replied, her eyebrows shooting up in shock at my suggestion.

'Ce n'est pas possible. The Lady Anne would very much like to be queen but the king already has one: Catherine of Aragon.'

Aha! That gave me a clue as to the time frame: this

must be before 1533 when Anne Boleyn finally got what she desired and married Henry and became Queen of England.

Anne was bitterly disappointed at the king's reaction when she bore him another daughter – who would incidentally go on to become Elizabeth l – and after three short years of marriage Anne Boleyn was executed in 1536. She was the second of the six wives married to the difficult Tudor monarch, who by the time of her death had already transferred his affections to another lady-in-waiting: the much loved Jane Seymour who gave him a cherished son.

But, of course, the Prioress didn't know any of this as it was all in the future. Ah, the wisdom of hindsight!

This small bejewelled woman, with her flirty French small talk, was the reason that besotted King Henry nearly led the country to war, fell out with the Pope and was excommunicated from the Catholic Church – a move which eventually led to the foundation of the Church of England. Well, well, what trouble she caused!

I glanced across at the courting pair again and I am sure I saw Lady Anne rubbing her neck.

The low boughs of the great yew tree sheltered the pair and kept to itself any whispered plans and royal secrets.

I snuck over within earshot and hid inside the great tree trunk listening to Lady Anne using a very wheedling tone interspersed with French words, telling the king that his marriage to Queen Catherine was not valid, because she had previously been married to his elder brother the crown prince Arthur, who died before he was crowned king. Henry put his head on one side. He seemed to like her persuasive argument.

Time to nip back down the time tunnel and return to the 21st century before things got nasty. I couldn't get the image of Lady Anne rubbing her neck out of my mind.

'Would you like to see what happened next?' asked Athelstan once I had safely returned, knowing my curiosity was torturing me.

'Come back tomorrow night then, Little Pup, and you can return to the scene a few years later and find out for yourself what happened from a far better narrator than I…'

When I scrambled out from the roots of the big yew tree the following night, I couldn't believe the sight which met my eyes. The dear little priory was now just a ruin. The gardens were overgrown, and everything that was removable had been taken. The former place of sanctuary was now a roofless shell.

I saw a cat strolling in the overgrown gardens and decided to try to speak to it rather than chase it. This cat might know what had happened.

The Secret Adventures of Rolo

'I am Araminta, looked after by the last prioress, Magdalen. She had to leave when the king's men closed down the priory. It broke her heart to leave me, but I thought she stood a better chance of seeking a new home somewhere if she travelled without me, so I hid in an outbuilding until she gave up looking for me. I can still hear her calling my name through her tears,' the cat added softly.

'Why did the priory close down? What on earth happened here?' I asked the cat, shocked at the crumbling state of the once lovely flint stone building.

'How long have you got?' asked Araminta, lying down on the weedy path in the afternoon sunshine next to the exterior wall and proceeding to lick her paws.

I sat next to her and waited patiently with my listening face on. Paws together and eyes closed. Araminta began,

'I don't know where you have been over the last couple of years, strange dog. Don't you know anything about the king breaking with the church in Rome after the Pope refused to say that his marriage to Queen Catherine was illegal, which would have left him free to marry Anne Boleyn?'

'I've been away for a bit,' I said quietly and she went on,

'Thomas Cromwell advised the king that he could set up his own branch of Christianity and call himself Supreme Head of the Church of England and this was passed as an Act of Parliament in 1534. Cromwell went on to further point out that the monasteries owned more land and wealth than anyone in the country, and there was nothing to stop Henry from seizing them for himself because they were loyal to the Pope. As new Head of the Church he could take all the spoils for the royal coffers once he had sold off the land to his loyal supporters.'

The cat paused for a moment and resumed her cleaning. I watched fascinated as her tongue working in rhythmical strokes over her paws. I thought it wise not to speak, as I didn't want to interrupt her flow in the telling of events since my last visit to

Ankerwycke.

'So about the same time that Queen Anne had her head removed from her body, king's men came to loot and close down the dear priory on the orders of Cromwell.

'They took the silver communion plate, furniture and candlesticks, destroyed the altar cloth and tapestries, and the terrified sisters fled the erstwhile place of sanctuary in fear for their lives. The gardens they had so lovingly tended were trampled underfoot and have since been choked by weeds as you can see.'

The cat suspended her narrative and we looked around at the once thriving garden now overgrown and indeed in a sorry state.

'So that was the end of it…' I murmured and Araminta piped up,

'Actually that was just the beginning… Queen Anne was executed on 19 May 1536 and the very next day King Henry was betrothed to Jane, another lady-in-waiting but much quieter than her predecessor

Anne. She was of the Seymour family from Wolf Hall in Wiltshire…'

Oh yes, I thought…I know where that is…not far from where I live with the smiley lady and floppy haired boy! It was rumoured that a tunnel was discovered underneath Wolf Hall leading to Tottenham House in Savernake, where Henry Vlll used to stay during hunting expeditions in the forest during his marriage to Anne Boleyn.

'Henry married Jane Seymour ten days after the execution, but she was never crowned queen. Now, little dog, you are up to date. Their son, Edward, was born just a week ago on 12th October. Now everyone is pleased; the king has a male heir and is very much in love with his wife Jane. All is well within the kingdom. Perhaps the king will now focus on his new family and stop closing down all the monasteries, convents and churches, and maybe my prioress will come back and find me and take me with her…'

I left the cat to her musings and took my leave. The problem with time travel was that you came with knowledge from the future.

How could I tell Araminta that the brief happiness enjoyed by the new royal family would be short–lived, as Jane would soon die of childbirth fever and her son was sickly?

Edward would be crowned king but he would not reign for long. Before that came to pass, the closing of religious houses would get a lot worse because King Henry needed the money to fund his military campaigns. Over time the old king would have three further queens by his side.

No, it was far better to leave the cat with her optimism and return to the calm of the house of the smiley lady and the floppy haired boy.

I went back to the wide yew tree.

Something on the back of my head was bothering me and I had to stop and sit down and scratch it every few steps. As you know, we dogs scratch with our back legs so this hindered my journey home.

At the foot of the Athelstan tree, I remembered

from a previous adventure that the Seymour family owned the land where Marlborough Castle once stood, so I asked Athelstan about that, as he knows a lot about local history and, well, let's face it, history in general.

'A house had been built on the site of the ruined castle after it fell into disrepair due to it no longer having any military significance. That house belonged to the crown and Henry Vlll gifted it to his new brother-in-law, Edward, upon the king's own marriage to Jane Seymour, and Edward became the first Duke of Somerset.

'The house was rebuilt in 1711 and fine gardens and a fashionable grotto were added in the 18th century as the house passed down the generations. When the 7th Duke of Somerset died in 1750, the fine house was leased out as a coaching inn. It became a very fashionable place to break the long road journey by carriage from London to Bath, for an overnight stay and to change the horses necessary to complete the journey, particularly during what was known as the 'season'.

'Travelling by carriage was not that comfortable and the road was nothing like the current A4 with its smooth tarmac surface. Ladies and gentlemen would travel to Bath during the summer months to get away from London. They took 'the mineral waters' from the Pump Room which they believed ensured good health, and they enjoyed many parties and dances whilst in the town.

During this period the house was called 'The Castle Inn' and for the following 90 years it opened its doors to such important visitors as the Duke of Wellington and Prime Minister William Pitt.

The rise of the railways in the 1840s led to the death of the stage coach business, just as the railways had seen off competition from the canals. The Castle Inn closed in January 1843 and was eventually transformed into Marlborough College for the education of sons from good families destined for the clergy.'

So there we are. A bit of local history according to Athelstan.

Dog blog #7 - According to Rolo

What an exciting and exhausting day out we've had today! The smiley lady took me to the Cotswold Wildlife Park near Burford.

She was so excited because dogs are actually allowed in there; as long as we dogs are kept on short leads that is. There are not many places that dogs are actually allowed to visit. And not only that, they didn't charge for me to go in!

I barked at the lady in the ticket booth because she leaned into the car and the smiley lady told me to be quiet. I was only introducing myself in case she didn't know who I was. The smiley lady said I would be banned if I carried on like that. I sat quietly and waited to

be let out from the car once we had
parked under a tree for shade in a
nearby field.

It was a beautiful sunny day near
the end of the summer term and
several school parties and play
groups were also enjoying a day
trip to the park.

The big old house and wonderful
formal gardens planted up with
marvellously colourful borders are
very impressive to the visitor.
Don't forget that I am not like
other dogs that can only see in
black and white — I can actually
appreciate the wonder of nature's
paint box in all its technicolour
glory.

The first animals we saw were birds;
mainly different types of owls. I

put my paws up on the barrier to
get a better look and they seemed
very interested indeed in me,
swivelling their heads and staring
at me with their beady eyes. I
wondered if they might know Bubo.

The smiley lady pulled me away
gently, because she was afraid the
owls might be eyeing me up as a
possible daytime snack. I wasn't
allowed into the big walk-in
aviary, nor the reptile house, not
even to see the bats. Pity, really,
but I do understand there are some
places it's just not safe for a
little dog to go.

I pulled the smiley lady towards
an interesting pen and was quickly
steered away again, but not before
I had the chance to read the label:
some sort of wild cat. Alas we were

not destined to meet.

Wandering across the park we found
an enclosure with giant tortoises
in it — I've never seen such big,
slow plodders! I would have liked
to go in and have a ride on one of
their backs, but again the smiley
lady pulled me away. ☹

Ooh! Then I spied a fishpond full
of brightly coloured water lilies,
just right for a cooling drink on a
hot summer's day. I nearly tipped
in head first, but luckily the
smiley lady had a firm hold of my
lead.

167

Another big grassy enclosure held
a group of camels with two humps.
Makes me wonder what the collective
noun for a group of camels is? A
hump?
The camels didn't take much notice
of me. Neither did the zebras.
I knew that a bunch of zebra is
called a dazzle. I also wondered
how the camels felt about being
in a field, thinking sand would be
their natural habitat.

Right in the middle of the park
we saw a family of white rhino in
a huge enclosure surrounded by a
wire fence and a moat to keep them
safe. They are HUGE and all have
a pointy horn on their heads. I
don't really understand why they
are called white rhino because they
are actually a kind of greeny-grey,
but the smiley lady didn't say the

The Secret Adventures of Rolo

answer to that one out loud so she probably doesn't know either. There was a really cute baby rhino called Ian who was only three months old. Rhino have wrinkly saggy bottoms. So does the smiley lady, but you didn't hear that from me. ☺

We came upon an anteater. What a funny looking animal with a very long nose. It looked like it might tip over with the weight of it. Then we saw a peacock with its tail feathers up, putting on a marvellous display. The peahens weren't very impressed but I was. I wondered if the show was especially for me, being a famous dog.

A little train whistled past full of waving children. I looked up at the smiley lady. I knew we both really wanted to ride on that narrow gauge train, so we set off at once to find the station.

The smiley lady paid the fare (again I travelled free) and we sat in one of the small open carriages. I climbed up on the wooden seat and sat on the smiley lady's lap because I didn't want to miss a thing! She moved me back onto the seat crossly because she was wearing white trousers and the paths are made of red sand so she was now covered in red paw prints! Oops. I decided to avoid eye contact and turned towards the window.

I heard the smiley lady say to a family with young children who were also riding on the train that the park hadn't changed since she used to bring her children here when

they were small. She said it was
harder work bringing me, though;
I don't know what she meant by
that. I was still scratching behind
my ear a fair bit but she hadn't
noticed.

Whooo! We trundled past the rhinos
and zebras and through the gardens
and suddenly saw some jolly tall
giraffes! If I closed my eyes really
tight I could imagine I was in
Africa, not Oxfordshire! I thought
to myself that the markings on a
giraffe resemble sun-baked African
soil in a drought.

We waved at lots of children
watching the train and they waved
back.

When we got back to the little
station, we walked past the school

children now enjoying their picnic lunches. I really wanted to go and hoover up after them, but again the smiley lady said no. She can be such a spoilsport.

No sign of the red panda. I was half expecting a big black and white cuddly teddy bear-type panda in the bamboo, but this one is small, presumably red and, today, not visible.

My favourite part of the whole park is the walled garden. This contains the Humboldt penguins and they have a really fun water slide into their cool blue pool and they live in little houses concealed amongst the rocks. I really, really wanted to jump over the low wall and have a swim with them, but the smiley lady held me tight and only let me put my paws up on the wall to watch for a minute or two.

I could have stayed there all day —
it was THAT exciting! The penguins
were playing chase and jumping in
the water and swimming about a bit
and then gliding out and shaking to
dry, just like I do when I've been
swimming in the river. I wondered
if they could play 'fetch' with a
ball. Probably not. I didn't think
their beaks would be wide enough
for a tennis ball.

In the next enclosure and just a

173

short step away from the penguins
were the meerkats. Boy oh boy did
they look fun! They stand up on
their hind legs — I can do that
too! There were quite a few meerkat
families with babies and the adults
were all standing up and staring at
me.

Quite rude, I thought. I started
squeaking at them in frustration
and trying to jump over the wall,
but the smiley lady pulled me away
again saying it was time to move
on. ☹

Wow! In the next pen were some
prairie dogs. Well, that's what the
label said, but they were tiny: not

174

dog-like at all — more like big gerbils. They looked as if they were also having lots of fun and I really wanted to go and play with them too — they were rolling in the dust and playing tag.

Yes, you've guessed it — I was steered out from the walled garden pretty sharpish and had a big drink of water from a thoughtfully provided doggy bowl.

I sat under a bench whilst the smiley lady ate an old-fashioned ice cream. I looked up hopefully, doing my best meerkat impression, and eventually she gave me the very end of the cone — not quite the bit I was after.

A final walk around the rhino paddock and then it was time to go home. What a lovely day out we both had. I love Cotswold Wildlife Park and I think it's open every day of the year except Christmas Day. I hope we visit again soon. I bet we both sleep well in our baskets tonight. ☺

Chapter 10

Rolo and the Gunpowder Plot

The next morning the smiley lady finally noticed that I was scratching my ear rather more than usual and she put her hand down to stroke me and felt a hard lump.

After an emergency visit to the vet – thankfully no sign of the kissing cat on the reception desk this time – I have to suffer the embarrassment of being sent home wearing a cardboard cone around my neck to stop me scratching my ear whilst the spot heals. Nothing more than an infected bite, the vet said, although which century I had been bitten in remained to be seen.

That night Yulia summoned me by the usual means of tapping on the kitchen window and she could barely suppress her giggles at the sight of me struggling through the trapdoor with the silly cardboard cone around my head.

Even Athelstan had to fight to keep his composure as he looked down from his woody perch. I suppose

I must look rather ridiculous. I tried to muster my dignity and ignore them.

'Early 17th century for you, Little Pup,' he tried to keep a straight face as he told me I was off to the Houses of Parliament.

'Do you want to take young Gwyn with you? He would love a time-travelling adventure. He's too young to fly just yet, but keep him out of mischief.'

Yulia held out what looked like a small leather bucket on a strap and I realised it was a kind of saddle bag for the transportation of the dragonling.

Rather than Gwyn being strapped to me, I was rather hoping it would be the other way round; I was looking forward to another dragon flight, but of course he was much too small to carry my weight and couldn't use his wings for flight just yet anyway.

I set off to find my young scaly charge and he came to the entrance of the quarry at once when called, hopping over the cave floor. Yulia set her lantern on the ground and held out the pouch and Gwyn jumped straight in eager for adventure and burbling

'Roro' which I assume was supposed to be me.

He snuggled down in the bottom of the bag and
Yulia and Da lifted it carefully between them and
tightened the girth strap around my middle. The
dragonling was loaded. We were all set.

I dropped the pink ball at the foot of the Athelstan
tree and we went off down the time tunnel.

Yulia and Da led the way and I could hear sniggering
from the woodland animals left behind in the forest.
We must have been quite a funny sight, a bit like a
pantomime horse.

I kept catching the cardboard collar on the sides
of the tunnel as it is quite narrow down there as
you know, and only wide enough to fit a slim Jack
Russell, not the silly appendage.

The Secret Adventures of Rolo

'It's just as well Gwyn can't breathe fire yet or he'd ignite your collar!' laughed Yulia.

Eventually we came out in some kind of store room and I wondered if we were in the right place. No sound from the bag, so I assumed Gwyn was sleeping.

Looking around, I could just about make out sacks of something: bundles of firewood and heaps of coal. It felt chilly. Not summer, that's for sure.

'Avast! What creature are you?' boomed a voice from the shadows. I couldn't pinpoint exactly where it was coming from, but with my sense of hearing sharpened in the gloom I thought I could detect a note of merriment. The pesky collar - I'd almost forgotten I was wearing it!

I edged forward cautiously, unsure of whom I was addressing and in front of me stepped a short man in a large floppy hat which almost covered his face, and he was completely wrapped in a large cloak.

There was a certain aroma about him, and I would say he'd been in this underground place without a wash for a good few days at least. I could see his breath as he spoke; it was that cold in there.

'Egad! What is that around your neck?' enquired the man.

'It's the latest fashion where I come from,' I said sarcastically, 'it's called a…ruff.'

Now, I should point out that I didn't actually say it was called a 'ruff', I merely turned in the direction of a scurrying sound I heard coming from the sacks and gave a little warning bark which probably sounded like 'ruff'.

Right on cue, Gwyn woke up and popped his little dragon head out from the leather bag. All talk of fashionable collars was completely forgotten.

The man jumped back in surprise and then his eyes narrowed, glinting in the dark as he saw the dragon.

'Ah good, you will come in very useful and no mistake!' he said.

'What are you doing down here anyway?' I asked

when the man reassured me that our only other companions were mice and rats.

'I am going to blow up the Houses of Parliament and everyone in it especially the King!' said the man quite matter-of-factly, as if it was a ridiculous question to be asking. I had no idea what I had got myself into; he had seemed at first to be a regular kind of guy.

The man patted the sack of corn next to him and I jumped up and settled down, keen to hear his story. Gwyn went back to sleep in his pouch.

'Since 1534 and the break with the true church in Rome under Henry Vlll we Catholics have had a bit of a hard time of things here.

'Edward Vl, the boy king, continued strengthening the Church of England from 1547 onwards, but when he died in 1553 Catholicism came back in favour during the reign of Queen Mary. She was the daughter of Catherine of Aragon and Henry Vlll and was a loyal Catholic. Unfortunately for us, her reign only lasted five years and she was replaced on the throne in 1558 by Queen Elizabeth l, who was very much her father's daughter; Catholicism was once more outlawed and Protestantism again became the order of the day.

'With the accession of James l (King James Vl of Scotland) after his cousin Elizabeth's death in 1603, there has been growing concern from powerful Spain about the growth and spread of Protestantism in Europe and all sorts of plots are hatching with a view to overthrowing King James and the new-fangled bible he had commissioned from the Puritans.

'The king declared that new parliament would meet early in the new year. The king himself would be present. It was time to act. My friends and I have

The Secret Adventures of Rolo

had enough of this anti-Catholic persecution and all the empty promises: we want a return to the true faith. We have made a plan to get rid of this Protestant king and his parliament once and for all and we have called our plot 'the great blow'.

'Who are your friends?' I asked, casually.

'Robert Catesby, Thomas Percy, Thomas Winter, John Wright and I hatched the plan in a room above the Duck and Drake Inn and now we have other loyal Catholic supporters coming on board. Robert Winter, John Grant and Christopher Wright and Ambrose Rookwood, Francis Tresham and Sir Everard Digby complete our merry band. 'Papists' they call us. We are being thwarted by Parliament, however, and they must suspect something is afoot because they keep postponing the date for the 'Opening of Parliament'. The latest information we have is that it is set for tomorrow which is 5th November 1605, with the king in attendance, so tonight I will put the finishing touches to our cunning plan.'

I thought I could hear my heart beating loudly in my

The Secret Adventures of Rolo

chest as I suddenly realised the danger that Gwyn and I were in. Surely this man was not going to let me escape now I knew his plan as well as the names of his accomplices? Now he was showing me the door that he would escape through. Think, Rolo, think!

'How are you planning to blow up this building then?' I asked as casually as I could.

'Look about you...' He swept his arm around indicating the piled sacks of grain. On closer inspection I realised that they were concealing barrels of gunpowder!

'We have smuggled 35 of these in here and most are already in place. Tonight I will lay a trail and, just before dawn, light the fuse. It will be a slow burn, and timed to perfection. Once the king is inside Parliament – BANG! – and if all goes according to plan the true faith will be restored throughout the realm.'

I could see the man's dark eyes glinting and knew that he was deadly serious.

'Only problem is, I have forgotten my tinder box and have no means of making a spark. Then, all at once, my prayers are answered and you bring me the creature that has the power to light the fuse!'

Oh no, I thought. This was surely not why Athelstan had sent us here: for Gwyn and yours truly to become conspirators in the Gunpowder Plot?!

Yulia had mentioned that Gwyn couldn't yet breathe fire, but of course this fire master wasn't to know that! I hoped very strongly that Gwyn wouldn't suddenly discover his flame throwing powers during our very dangerous visit to the cellars of the Houses of Parliament!

l glanced down at the dragon and realised he had no idea what was going on, although he was now awake, he just sat there blinking in his bag. It seemed he hadn't yet developed the power to read minds either.

'Sssssh! There is someone coming!' He grabbed me by the collar and held me tightly, my face stuffed into his sweaty cloak.

'Who goes there?'

I already had an ear up and knew someone had entered the vaults of the building.

'Robert, Kit and John!' came three gruff voices in the dark.

My captor let go of me and asked in a low voice what they wanted, as they had all agreed NOT to meet up until after the event to avoid raising suspicion.

'What is that little dog wearing around his neck?' asked one of the men catching sight of me.

'It's called a ruff. Never mind that now. What are you doing here? You know what we agreed,' said the man.

'We have a problem,' said another voice.

'Someone has written a letter to a member of parliament advising him not to attend tomorrow's state Opening of Parliament,' said another.

'It must be Francis! He's related by marriage to Monteagle and must have warned him to stay away.

I knew we shouldn't have trusted him,' piped up the third man. They all sounded pretty nervous to me. Wild accusations were flying around the room.

'What are we going to do?'

'If the ceremony hasn't been called off, then we will go ahead as planned. Everything is in place. I will light the fuse tonight ; it will take hours to follow my carefully laid trail to the main store of explosive, right underneath the chamber.'

The cloaked man sounded confident and the other three were satisfied and left the building, having crossed themselves and wished each other 'God Speed'. I wished I could follow them.

The next couple of hours were spent keeping a low profile, watching the man tipping barrel after barrel of powder and rolling it carefully to lay a line that would act as a fuse to the pile he wanted to blow.

Then the moment I had been dreading arrived. He seized Gwyn roughly by the neck, pulling him out from my pouch and entreated the dragonling to breathe fire and light the fuse.

The Secret Adventures of Rolo

The startled dragon blinked and gasped a couple of times and the man squeezed him a bit tighter, muttering incoherently.

I hardly dared look through my paws, as I thought the poor dragon was being strangled. Then the thing I least expected actually happened: Gwyn the dragonling produced the tiniest spark and at once the man pushed the dragon's face roughly towards the ground and told him to do it again.

This time there was a fizz and a flare and the fuse was lit. It didn't seem to travel at all. It must have been set to a very slow burn indeed; either that or there was something wrong with the powder. But I

189

didn't fancy hanging around to see.

The man rubbed his hands together with glee and kissed the surprised dragon on the top of his little scaly head. Then he set him down on the floor and I shepherded him back into the bag for safety, where he sat spluttering and regaining his breath. I expect he was feeling pretty pleased with himself without having any idea of what he had just facilitated. The man was heading for the door that would probably take him outside to freedom. He didn't give me a second glance.

I wondered what my best course of action was. A quick glance at the fuse reassured me that it didn't seem to be travelling very fast… well, if the king wasn't expected in the building until eleven o'clock the next day, then the arsonist would be anticipating about 12 hours of slow burn.

Suddenly the underground store room was filled with light and two burly armoured men carrying flaming torches appeared from a passage way. They seemed mighty surprised to see a small dog wearing a stupid cone around its head. Without wanting to waste any more time, I shouted a warning about the gunpowder and pointed to the door where the man had just pretty sharply exited the scene.

Left alone with the slow burning fuse, whilst the guards pursued the fleeing man, I did what comes most naturally to me in the whole world – yes, I'm afraid I wee'd on it and was pleased to see the tiny flame went out with a sizzle, just as I thought it would!

I just hoped those men were going to be careful with their flaming torches with all that gunpowder lying about! Goodness knows how far the fuse ran or where the bulk of the explosives lay.

'Stop in the name of the king! You are under arrest!' was the last thing I heard as I fled the scene with Gwyn bouncing in his leather pannier, heading as fast as my paws would carry us to the time tunnel where Yulia and Da were waiting. I certainly didn't want to be caught with the smoking gun!

'What was the outcome? Do you know whether they caught the plotters?' I asked Athelstan later, once I

The Secret Adventures of Rolo

had seen Gwyn back to the safe haven of the quarry. The hatchling was exhausted after such an exciting adventure and would soon be fast asleep on his nest.

'Yes, Little Pup,' said the wise tree guardian,

'A man calling himself John Johnson was arrested trying to leave the storeroom by royal officials Sir Thomas Knyvett and Edward Doubleday, but the man's real name turned out to be Guy Fawkes. The rest of the conspirators were either shot as they fled or later rounded up and captured, tried and then executed for treason.

To ensure this never happened again, there is always a thorough search of the basement before the State Opening of Parliament, although these days it is more of a ceremonial search by the Beefeaters.'

'By the way, I think you should know that Gwyn has discovered how to breathe fire. It's just a little spark at the moment...' I dropped in casually, and made my way wearily to bed, still wearing the stupid collar or should I say 'ruff'.

I will try to remember this adventure on 5th

The Secret Adventures of Rolo

November, when the floppy haired boy and his friends celebrate Guy Fawkes failing to blow up the Houses of Parliament, by setting off fireworks in our back garden.

As in previous years, I will be kept indoors and will no doubt bark angrily through the curtains. I don't like fireworks, as you know, because of the noise they make, but at least now I know what it's all about.

Dog Blog #8 - According to Rolo

It was a lovely warm and sunny June day and the smiley lady bundled me in the car and we drove a short distance to a nearby hill; the highest viewpoint in Wiltshire. Here we met up with some other ladies and their dogs; two bouncy Dalmatians and a more sedate springer Spaniel.

The ladies started talking and we

four dogs had a marvellous game of playing chase in the long grass on the chalk downs, rolling in the red clover and buttercups. There were brightly patterned red and black moths flitting from flower to flower. It was a long walk for the ladies and the nettles were growing high in places. The smiley lady had three-quarter length trousers on — that was a bit silly, I thought.

Their collective orientation skills left a bit to be desired, but we dogs just carried on playing and running ahead. Every time we reached a cattle trough the bigger dogs would stop and lean in for a drink. I wasn't quite tall enough but I managed to put my paws up and just about reach. This caused great hilarity. Then the older Dalmatian Charlie and I started a great game where he would carry his chain lead and I would wrestle it off him. He'd give it to me quite easily and then, once I'd won, I would drop it and he would pick it up again. This passed the time quite happily as we crossed yet another field.

The ladies were getting rather concerned as to whether they were walking back to the car park in the right direction and we were forging our way through a very overgrown meadow, convinced it was parallel to the path we had started out on. I got fed up with following as I couldn't see over the tall grass, so I went off on my own to explore. I found a very deep and inviting hole hidden in the side of the hill just off the path. The entrance was hidden by the long grass. The earth smelt fresh and exciting. I didn't

hesitate and went in head first.
It was a maze of secret tunnels and
I hoped it was the badger family
I helped escape from the forest
last year. I just wanted to find out
if they were settled in their new
secret home.

I didn't realise at the time, but
heard what was happening above
ground later on when the smiley
lady was telling the story to the
floppy haired boy:

'My heart was in my mouth. I
suddenly realised Rolo wasn't with
the other dogs. For a full ten
minutes I had no idea where he was.
I called him and called him and
retraced my steps. Then I caught
a glimpse of a well-disguised
badger sett just visible in the
grass. My heart sank because, as

you know, badger setts are magnets
to terriers but can also be death
traps. I called the other ladies
over and we all kept calling his
name over and over again.

'Suddenly Rolo appeared in the
hole, but ignored us and didn't
come out; just casually walked past
the entrance. Twice more he did
this but at least I knew now where
he was. All sorts of nightmares
were running through my mind:

what if the daddy badger fought
with him? Supposing he got stuck
and couldn't turn around to come
out? I would have to get a shovel
from somewhere quickly and start
digging… I was really panicking.
'Meanwhile, one of the walkers, a
very petite French lady, jumped
into the entrance of the hole. She

asked me to pass her Rolo's lead
and a dog biscuit. She clipped the
biscuit onto the end and dangled it
in the tunnel and when he appeared
and sniffed it she grabbed his
collar and hoiked him out and put
him in my arms. I buried my face
in his fur which smelt of damp
earth. I was so angry but also very
relieved and quickly attached his
lead to his collar, not wishing to
take any more chances.'

'Oh mum, how frightening! You must
keep a closer eye on him and not be
so busy chatting when you're out
walking!' said the floppy haired boy
seriously.

I was sorry I had scared the
smiley lady so much. How could
she know that I knew the badger
family who lived in that sett and

The Secret Adventures of Rolo

I just wanted to visit and pay my respects?

I had spoiled the lovely walk and finished it very firmly on the lead and eventually the smiley lady calmed down and forgave me. I licked her under the chin a lot to show I was sorry.

Chapter 11

Rolo and the 13th Horoscope

It was late in the day on a sunny summer afternoon. The smiley lady went up to Marlborough College observatory with a group to see the famous Blackett's telescope: the largest refracting telescope in Wiltshire.

I went along too.

Whilst the ladies were all chatting outside waiting for the group to assemble, I glanced up at the sky and wondered what on earth they were expecting to see with the sun still shining brightly. I thought a telescope was for observing the night sky.

Suddenly I saw an upside down rainbow; well more of a saucer really. It was a thin curved line with the seven colours of the prism: red, orange, yellow, green, blue, indigo and violet. I ran around in circles excitedly wagging my tail.

'Shhhh, Rolo. Calm down. There's a good boy,' admonished the smiley lady, patting me and immediately going back to her chatter as she untangled my lead from her legs.

'Look at that!' noticed one of the ladies, pointing to the saucer in the sky.

The professor from the college said,

'Goodness gracious, I've never seen one of those before and I've been here for 18 years! It's a Zenithal Arc.' He said excitedly and immediately got his mobile phone out to share the phenomenon with local astronomers.

'Excuse me, I saw it first,' I wanted to shout, but nobody was listening.

They were all trying very hard not to look directly at the sun because everyone knows it can damage your eyes, but they also wanted to look at this rare occurrence.

Suddenly I noticed the Zenithal Arc was not alone up there; it was flanked by two smaller prisms. The professor saw them at exactly the same time as me,

'Sun dogs!' he shouted excitedly and the ladies all looked towards the heavens, forgetting NOT to look directly at the sun.

'Even the Ancient Greeks knew about sun dogs' he explained. 'Aristotle wrote that the sun was flanked by two mock suns which always stay beside it and never try to overtake it, and they are only usually visible at this time of year at sunrise or towards sunset.'

I couldn't work out why they were called sun dogs as they looked like little bursts of rainbow to me, but it seems the professor read my thoughts because he explained that the term possibly came from a corruption of a word in Norfolk where 'dag' meant 'dew or mist' and the sighting of a sun dog was seen as a forewarning of bad weather.

Actually it is the formation of hexagonal ice crystals refracting the light, but I am sure he knows this and will duly share his knowledge with the ladies.

I'd like to have said something profound and intelligent to this academic and all I could think of

The Secret Adventures of Rolo

was an old Swedish saying, 'The afternoon knows what the morning never expected' – but of course he couldn't hear my words of great wisdom.

Well weren't we lucky? A whole bunch of astronomical phenomena going on all at once!

The ladies put on special 3D glasses and were told to look down at the ground first and then sweep their gaze upward to give their retinas time to adjust so as not to be damaged by the dazzle of the sun.

The smiley lady said that instead of the usual glare, the sun looked like a red orb. This must have been for my benefit as I wasn't given any special glasses to wear. I had to wait until they had finished looking through them. Then it was time to go inside the strange round building with a copper roof to peer through the telescope.

The copper roof itself is amazing as it opens with a pulley system and looks very much like a Heath Robinson invention.

The telescope is magnificent and shiny. It is made mainly of bronze and is one of the original telescopes made by Thomas Cooke of York in 1860 for Mr Joseph Gurney Barclay and professional astronomers. It spent many years pointing to the heavens above the Radcliffe in Oxford, but when that observatory relocated to South Africa the telescope was purchased for Marlborough College in 1935, where it remained in a poor state of repair.

In 1997 it was rebuilt, restored and modernised under the watchful eye of our guide, Professor Barclay who, when researching the history of the telescope, discovered he was actually related to the Barclay for whom the telescope was originally made.

I dozed off on the carpet whilst the ladies took turns to climb a rickety step ladder and peer through the eyepiece to see the red dot of the sun. No chance of me getting up there for a look with this lot around, I thought.

Professor Barclay was talking about the signs of the zodiac: Aries, Taurus, Gemini, Cancer, Leo, Virgo, Libra, Scorpio, Sagittarius, Capricorn, Aquarius and Pisces, and their position in the night sky at various times of the year and when they are in their ascendant and so on. Then I pricked up my ears. He mentioned the 13th zodiac called Ophiuchus.

'Strange things happen during the period from 30th November to 18th December,' he was saying. Now that got my attention.

'Zodiac means 'circle of animals'. The zodiac assigned to each person depends on which constellation was behind the sun, and therefore visible from earth, on the day that person was born.

'Accordingly, it is said that certain signs have dominant traits which may affect your personality. The Earth is affected by the gravitational pull of the moon and the sun and therefore positions are a little out of kilter from when they were mapped by the ancient astrologers.

'If you look at the night sky in the 21st century, you might expect to see the stars of your zodiac sign most clearly around your birthday at night or during an eclipse, as that is the time they are behind the sun and therefore most visible from Earth.

'However, because of the continual drifting of the stars, the heavenly calendar is about a month out and what will be most prominent is the neighbouring constellation.' He paused, allowing the ladies to take all this in. I could see that this talk of astrology and astronomy was mostly going over their heads.

However, this was very exciting stuff to me – a bit like the sundial on the church which is an hour out, the whole astrology map is about a month out! I wondered if the two had any relevance to each other. The professor expanded this theory,

'Two thousand years ago the 13th constellation was deliberately left out of the astrological zodiac and no one really knows why, but it is thought that because the 360 degree path of the sun neatly divides into 12, with each part equalling 30 degrees, it was incorporated into the other signs.

'Yet the sun passes in front of Ophiuchus AFTER it passes its neighbour Scorpio, and shields it for a full 19 days before it passes in front of Sagittarius,' the professor went on to explain, 'so it is definitely a very important but seemingly forgotten constellation.'

Wow! That's really got me thinking. I wonder if people who were born during those 19 days have different personality traits to either Scorpions or Sagittarians? The ladies debated this question and thoroughly enjoyed their visit to the Marlborough Telescope.

The Secret Adventures of Rolo

Dog Blog #9 - According to Rolo

You may recall that the smiley lady sings with a community choir. I know most of the songs because she plays the learning CD when we are on long journeys in the car and I think I could probably sing the 'middle' part with her.

It was choir practice night and the smiley lady was very concerned that I hadn't had much in the way of walkies that day and she was already running late.

Most unusually for a Wednesday night — I'm often left at home when she goes singing — she grabbed my lead and we half-walked and half-ran down to the redundant church in the High Street.

The other choir members were already in full song and they were delighted to see me precede the smiley lady.

I wagged my tail a lot and she tied me to a chair leg as she made her way to join the 'middle voice' section of the choir. I was tethered near the Chilvester Passage entrance, but luckily nobody noticed the portrait of me in the brickwork on the wall.

The Secret Adventures of Rolo

I wasn't quite close enough to make the passage way open by my presence, which was just as well or my secret route to London may have been revealed to forty singers!

I settled down with my head on my paws and the smiley lady joined her fellow singers in the nave. I perked up when they sang a rousing African song. They are practising hard for the upcoming Jazz Festival. Wonder if I'll go to it again this year?

One of the songs they sing has a line in it about cats and some of the singers make a cat noise — a 'miaow' and a 'tssss' like a hissing cat. That really woke me up and I jumped up at once, nearly pulling the chair over. I hope I wasn't too much of a distraction.

The singers were supposed to keep their eyes on their leader at all times for musical direction, but of course they were looking behind her to me. I loved all the ear ruffling and fuss I received afterwards, and then we walked home.

Chapter 12

Rolo and the Crown Jewels

During the summer months when the Queen is on holiday at Balmoral, her residence in Scotland, Buckingham Palace opens its doors to paying visitors. You can go in the state rooms and there is a different exhibition held every year.

The smiley lady was going up to London to have a tour of the palace and gardens and she was really looking forward to it; she had booked it sometime in advance as it is a popular day out, especially to foreign visitors.

The floppy haired boy asked her if she would see the crown jewels on display and she replied no, because they were kept under lock and key in the Tower of London.

'Pussy cat, pussy cat where have you been? I've been up to London to visit the Queen' she sang as she swept me up in her arms.

What a stupid rhyme! She went off to catch the

coach.

Being the summer holidays, the floppy haired boy was not at school and he promised his mum he would look after me. However, when his friends called round to see if he wanted to go and play tennis with them, he ushered me out into the garden and told me to do a wee. I saw him pick up his tennis racquet and his skateboard from the hallway beside the front door (where he still kept it despite being told by the smiley lady hundreds of times to keep it in his bedroom or in the garage). Then he shut me in the kitchen with the window open to let some air in.

I knew he wouldn't miss me and anyway he wasn't a very good timekeeper; the smiley lady often joked that he must have been off sick the day they learned to tell the time at school.

As soon as I heard the slam of the front door, I opened the cupboard under the sink and used my terrier escape hatch under the fence to get out of the garden and I ran down the road, just behind the floppy haired boy. There weren't too many people about because being the summer holidays families were already out for the day, enjoying the sunshine.

St Peter's redundant church in the High Street was already open for morning coffee, but my luck was in because no one noticed me entering the building.

I gingerly approached the outline of myself depicted in the brickwork on the wall behind the grand piano – the entrance to the Chilvester Passage. I knew it would take me to an exit behind a café sign quite close to Trafalgar Square.

As soon as I drew near enough, the lines around the portrait went fuzzy and I found myself inside the tunnel.

Luckily there was still a torch on the ground where I had left it from a previous adventure.

I was soon standing in the familiar noisy and bustling street, leaving the passage behind me sealed when the Talbot Café sign closed behind me with a bang.

I had arrived in London.

The Secret Adventures of Rolo

I made my way round the corner to Trafalgar Square.

A quick glance at the Fourth Plinth and I was surprised to see it was no longer home to a blue cockerel, but had the model of a skeleton of a horse. No time now to find out what that was all about.

I knew Buckingham Palace wasn't far away. I ran along Pall Mall, past St James's Palace, across the corner of Green Park – it only took me about 15 minutes to run all the way. I pride myself on being quite fit as little dogs go.

I saw the smiley lady pass the ticket booth into the garden, but luckily she didn't see me. I can spot her lime green mac a mile away. She was talking to someone; I wasn't really surprised; she does that wherever she goes.

In a long line of French windows I saw one that was open, and, after a quick glance about to make sure I was unobserved, I sneaked inside the palace.

I found myself in a library filled with floor to ceiling bookcases stuffed full of books, and, all around, occasional tables and leather arm chairs and a big desk probably for writing very important letters on crested notepaper.

A door opened and two Corgis came bounding into the room.

Okay, that's a bit of an exaggeration because they don't really bound, they waddle.

Funny dogs really, but highly favoured by the royal family. I believe the Queen was given one as a little girl and has owned her descendants ever since.

The royal dogs were followed by a footman, who sat in the important chair behind the desk and spread out the Racing Post to read.

The Corgis were oblivious to me at one end of the room, where I was hiding beneath one of the low tables.

'Psst,' I said, trying to get their attention. They didn't look vicious at all. Perhaps Corgis get a bad press; they are supposed to be working dogs, used for herding livestock in Wales where I too originated from. These two looked as if they had never done a day's work in their lives.

One of the Corgis let out a little squeak and the footman said,

'Be quiet Myrtle, there's a good girl. I'm checking my horses.'

The boy dog said in a very posh voice,

'I say, what on earth are you?' I looked about but, as I was the only one in range, presumed he was talking to me.

'My name's Rolo and I'm a time-travelling dog who loves history and nature,' I said proudly, by way of introduction. I am a dog of impeccable manners.

Both Corgis edged closer and the one who spoke was clearly impressed,

'Really? I say, I've always wanted to time travel! Can I come with you? The name's Knave, by the way.'

He seemed a bit star struck and I was visualising #roloismyhero on social media. I smiled kindly,

'Yes, sure, where do you want to go?'

'Now then, Knave, you know we shouldn't talk to strange dogs,' whined Myrtle.

Knave looked disdainfully at his companion and then turned towards me,

'I want to go back to the time when the crown jewels were nearly stolen,' he said emphatically. Maybe he thought he could do something about it?

'Now look here, Knave, I'm not sure we can actually influence the outcome of events, but we can certainly observe. I'll have to clear it first with Athelstan.'

'Who's he? Your master?' asked Knave.

'Not exactly, it's a bit complicated, but if you're serious about coming with me we had better get a move on. Are you sure you can get away from the palace without being missed?'

Well, so much for me looking round the state rooms; if this royal Corgi wanted adventure we would have to exit pretty sharpish.

'Myrtle, can you cover for me?'

'Well, I really don't think you should....'

Without further ado, I found myself leading the way through the French door and running across the manicured lawn with the stocky Corgi following on behind. The footman didn't even look up from his paper and appeared to be speaking to a bookmaker on the telephone placing bets on the afternoon's races.

By the time we got back to Trafalgar Square, Knave was panting quite heavily. I doubted his royal pudginess had ever had so much exercise! He seemed fascinated by the pigeons, but didn't want to chase them. He barked a lot. To be fair he'd probably had a bit of a sheltered life. I couldn't begin to imagine what it would be like to be a royal dog.

We passed the lamp post where the stolen painting from the National Gallery was once hidden, and crossed the road to the Talbot Café. I had to hold up the sign with my paw and revealed to Knave the Chilvester Passage.

'Wow,' was all he could say.

I must admit I hadn't really thought this plan through. It seemed a jolly good idea at the time, having an adventure with a royal dog.

There were, however, a few obstacles: for one, where was I going to hide a Corgi until night time? And two, what if Athelstan didn't let him into the time tunnel? And the third one occurred to me as I watched him struggle to squeeze through the gap: what if Knave didn't actually fit?

Luckily the journey home was uneventful save a lot of whining about being hungry. I used my torch and led the way.

We left St Peter's church unnoticed and Knave panted all the way up the hill. It was no good; he just wouldn't fit through the terrier escape hatch into my garden.

This didn't bode well for our time travelling adventure later.

I had to think on my feet, and instead led him to the forest and to the Athelstan tree. The poor Corgi was almost on his knees by this point.

'Well, well, Little Pup, who have we here?' asked Athelstan, emerging from the bark.

I introduced Knave and Athelstan gave a little bow when I explained who he was and what we wanted to do. The tree dragon scratched his head and said,

'You'd better leave him here with me and come back a bit later when you can get away from your people.'

I ran home, squeezing myself under the gate and back through the trapdoor just before the floppy

haired boy appeared, out of breath, thirsty and
without too much guilt about having left me home
alone for a few hours. He gave me a biscuit after a
cursory glance to make sure I hadn't wee'd anywhere
and then he flopped in front of the television and I
sat on his lap.

'You don't really want a walk do you, Rolo?' he said
as he gave me a belly rub.

The phone rang and it was the smiley lady ringing to
say she was going to stay overnight with the floppy
haired boy's big brother – the one with the rabbit
– who lives in London; I had a feeling that my plan
might just work.

The floppy haired boy gave me my tea, took me
out on my lead for ten minutes and shut me in the
kitchen saying he was going to a friend's house to
play on his Xbox.

I waited to hear the click of the front door and
off I went as fast as I could, through the trapdoor
and back to the Athelstan tree. It was quite empty
in the cupboard under the sink and I suddenly

The Secret Adventures of Rolo

remembered I had borrowed the bucket.

As I approached the oak tree, I could hear Athelstan and Knave laughing and sharing stories. I must admit I felt a bit jealous.

I heard Athelstan say that 'Corgi' was welsh for 'little dog' and they had been brought to Wales by Flemish weavers to herd livestock.

This one didn't look as if it could herd anything, I thought, except possibly a cream tea.

'Ah, there you are Little Pup. Just getting to know young Knave here a little better. What an interesting chap! Ready for your adventure? Look after him, won't you?'

We both nodded. I thought that the Corgi looked well rested and not so out of breath.

As I predicted, the time tunnel was going to be a challenge. Yulia produced another orb from somewhere, but getting the Corgi to 'drop' was proving difficult.

She wrestled it off him for the third time, shoved him towards the entrance and threw the orb down the hole to open the time tunnel. I followed, and then realised I couldn't get past him so had to allow him to go first. Yulia was giggling as she held her lantern high. She crawled through his legs so she could light the way ahead.

A couple of times the tunnel was a bit tight, and it was just as well I was at the rear. Yulia put her lantern down on the ground and squeezed back underneath the Corgi's legs to aid with the pushing. I put my shoulder in and heaved with all my might.

Three times we had to go through this pantomime. I made a mental note not to allow Knave to eat anything on our adventure or we'd never get him

The Secret Adventures of Rolo

back to the 21st century!

'Whereabouts do you sleep in the palace?' I asked, trying to strike up a conversation.

'We have our own room with wicker baskets and a daily menu is posted on the wall for our meals. What day is it today?' Knave asked.

'Tuesday,' Yulia replied.

'Oh well, I'm missing chuck steak today then. Maybe Myrtle will save me some. It will be rabbit tomorrow and poached chicken the day after, usually served with cabbage and rice. We have buttered scones for our tea, served by footmen in royal livery,' the Corgi sighed.

I had to admit this all sounded delicious. I quite fancied being a royal dog at least for a day. I wondered if Her Majesty would notice a Jack Russell in the pack?

During our journey, Yulia gave us a bit of background about the man who had tried to steal the crown jewels.

'Thomas Blood was an Irishman. He came to England to fight for King Charles l during the English Civil War, but when he saw the royalists were losing he switched sides and supported the roundheads under Oliver Cromwell.

'In 1660, when Charles ll was restored to the throne, Blood fled to Ireland with his family. He plotted further mischief with other exiled Cromwellians and, after a botched kidnapping in Ireland, he returned to England and set up as a doctor under an assumed name. There he hatched a plot to steal the crown jewels. He knew they were kept in the basement of the Tower of London, behind a metal grille.

'Disguised as a clergyman, 'Parson Blood' befriended the Keeper of the Jewels: a man called

Talbot Edwards who lived in the Tower above the basement with his family.

'After a visit to see the crown jewels with her husband, Mrs Blood feigned an illness and was taken to the Edwards' apartment to 'recover'. By way of thanks, 'Parson' Blood send a gift the following day thus inveigling his way into Talbot Edwards' trust and friendship.

'Athelstan is sending you to witness a meeting between Charles ll and Thomas Blood after his failed attempt to steal the Crown Jewels.' Knave was a bit disappointed as he wanted to witness the failed 'theft', but Athelstan probably thought the Corgi would be a bit of a liability and had wisely decided to send us to a point in time after the event.

Knave started barking for no apparent reason and Yulia waved us off with a glance of sympathy to me. He really would have to control all that barking, he was doing my furry little head in.

We were inside the Tower of London and it was 1671, not a year that I had ever visited before.

This was a private audience room and the first thing I noticed was a man sporting a long black curly wig and fine clothes and an air of importance, seated behind a desk.

Opposite him stood a man dressed not so richly but not shabbily either, with his hands bound behind his back. His head was held high and his demeanour was not the penitent stance you might expect of a captive, especially of a man caught in the act of stealing the Crown Jewels.

There were two other aristocratic gentlemen seated in the room, both wearing long curly wigs.

Must be awfully hot under all that hair, I thought.

Two guards stood at ease. Luckily no one spotted us. I was praying Knave would have the sense to keep quiet.

My eye was drawn down to the fine carpet and then I detected movement under the table.

There sprawled three King Charles Spaniels, all vying for position lying across the most important

The Secret Adventures of Rolo

gentleman's feet. Knave had seen them too. He looked most indignant and I warned him with a look not to start barking at them.

'I am descended from the first royal dog and she was a Corgi named Susan. What are these Spaniels doing here at the feet of the monarch?' the Corgi whispered unhappily.

So this was King Charles was it? I had to point out in hushed tones that we were about 350 years prior to the first Corgi at Buckingham Palace, so technically these were royal dogs. Really, this dog seemed to have very little brain, for all his royal standing.

The king stood up.

'So, Blood, my guards tell me that you will only confess your crime to your sovereign. Is that right, you scoundrel? What's to stop me executing you right now, here in the Tower for your impertinence?' he boomed at the prisoner.

The man looked King Charles straight in the eye and drew himself up to full height, answering in a lilting Irish brogue without any hint of subservience,

229

'I think you have been swindled, Sire, for these Crown Jewels that you believe to be worth £100,000 are only worth £6,000 maximum!' his eyes twinkled as he spoke.

I cringed inwardly, thinking it was never a good idea to challenge your king, but to my surprise King Charles banged his fist down on the table and roared with laughter. The better looking man of the trio stepped forward.

'Rupert, what shall we do with him?' the king said, turning to him.

The man called Rupert addressed the captive,

'Tell me you rogue, why were you trying to stuff the orb down your breeches?'

Orb? This confused me. Did the thief also have the means to time travel then?

'I was trying to have them valued, Sire.'

'Enough!' bellowed the third nobleman, who it transpired was the Duke of York.

'My men tell me that you and your brother-in-law and two accomplices gained the trust of our man Edwards and took advantage of that trust when you followed him to the cellar, watched him remove the grille and then stabbed him with your sword and beat him with a mallet knocking the poor man unconscious. Then you removed the mace, sceptre and orb and made off with them! Luckily my men restrained you at the Iron Gate.

'What do you have to say for yourself?' said the king and the twinkle in his eyes almost matched that of the restrained man.

'Well, no harm was done and you have them back; I was only trying to prove how easy it was to steal them,' said the audacious felon.

Prince Rupert exploded,

'What do you mean 'no harm was done'? Apparently your brother-in-law tried to saw through the sceptre because it wouldn't fit in the bag! You had the orb down your breeches and where was the crown? Flattened with a mallet!'

The Secret Adventures of Rolo

'Enough,' roared King Charles as the monarch rose to his feet.

The three noblemen had a whispered discussion in the corner of the room. The King then stood in front of Thomas Blood and addressed him directly,

'What if I should give you your life?'

Blood replied humbly, 'I would endeavour to deserve it, Sire!'

'Good answer, man. I was once advised to keep my friends close and my enemies closer and with this in mind I am going to let you off and grant you a pension. I will expect to see you at Court occasionally where I can keep my eye on you. You are banned, however, from coming within ten yards of the Crown Jewels for I don't trust you one jot!'

Prince Rupert and the Duke of York couldn't believe their ears and yet they knew their sovereign had a liking for this Irishman who was not afraid to speak out. The man had also highlighted the need for greater security of the Crown Jewels.

Oblivious to the drama, the Spaniels continued to sleep at the king's feet, not noticing our presence. The captive's hands were untied by the guards and the men were making jokes about the luck of the Irish. Knave looked like he was about to say something.

I dragged him outside and then the complaining started,

'I wanted to be a hero and catch the thief with the crown on his head! We missed the good bit. I'm hungry, what is there to eat?'

I ushered him back to the time tunnel before his yapping led to our discovery. Yulia rolled her eyes at me because Knave was still complaining all the way back to the forest.

Athelstan finished the story,

'Talbot Edwards, the keeper of the jewels, made a full recovery and kept his job. He was also rewarded with a pension and often retold the story to visitors to the Tower, embellishing his role, no doubt. Security around the jewels was greatly tightened.'

Athelstan added, 'It's as well Gwyn wasn't with you on this adventure as dragons will go to great lengths to acquire jewels, although I doubt he has discovered the lure of them just yet.'

'Knave, you had better get back to the Palace pretty sharpish as I am sure your friend Myrtle will be struggling to hide your disappearance,' I said.

'But I haven't had my supper,' wailed the tubby Corgi.

'No time for that now; Rolo will see you to the Chilvester Passage. I presume you can find your way home from there?' Athelstan spoke firmly.

The headlines of the Evening Standard the next day told of a Corgi from the palace found wandering about in Trafalgar Square. The Queen was greatly relieved to have her boy back and said she didn't know what he'd been up to and that he didn't seem to have come to any harm but that he was 'very hungry indeed.'

Dog Blog #10 — According to Rolo

When we are out walking I like to entertain the smiley lady. She thinks it's really funny every time I see a squirrel. They are often to be seen running along the top of a fence or even on the ground, but whenever they see me they scarper pretty sharpish up the nearest tree.

I stand up on my back legs barking at the squirrel and making my baby seal noise. I only do it to make her laugh; of course I know I cannot climb a tree after the pesky creature, but I do like to put on a good show.

I also made her laugh when she went out into the garden to fill the bird feeder with peanuts and she spilled quite a few on the patio. Quick as

a wink, I hoovered them all up.
Maybe we could evolve this into
some kind of act for 'Britain's Got
Talent', what do you think?

The Secret Adventures of Rolo

Chapter 13

Rolo and the Chocolate Factory

The floppy haired boy has history homework: to find out what happened in the year 1937.

He opened up his laptop and used a search engine to research historic events from that year. They included things like: the invention of Sellotape, Sir Frank Whittle's testing of the first jet engine, the publication of J.R.R. Tolkien's 'The Hobbit', the first BBC broadcast from Wimbledon tennis tournament, and the first 999 emergency telephone call.

He was telling the smiley lady all of these interesting facts and she said,

'I seem to remember my mum telling me that she was 6 years old when Rolo sweets first appeared in the shops. That would have been 1937. You know, the chocolate covered toffee sweets in tubes, always wrapped in gold foil.'

'Of course I know, mum, they are the sweets Rolo is named after because of his toffee and chocolate-covered face!'

I was pretending to be asleep, stretched out under the dining room table with my head on my paws but with an ear up, listening to this conversation.

I wanted to shout out,

'Actually floppy haired boy you are wrong! The sweets were named after me!' but of course I couldn't make him hear me.

So instead I will share the story with you.

The year is indeed 1937 and Athelstan had sent me via the time tunnel to a chocolate factory. I didn't have any tubby Corgis with me nor a fire-breathing dragon, not even my little friend Chickpea. It was just yours truly so you will have to take my word for what happened.

I emerged from the time tunnel in a vast kitchen filled with the wonderful aromas of melting chocolate. My nose was twitching with excitement.

I hid underneath a big vat and filled my nostrils with

The Secret Adventures of Rolo

the mouth-watering scent. There is nothing quite like it in the whole world!

A new lady had arrived to join the workforce. She introduced herself as Rene to the others. The bossiest of the ladies started explaining to Rene about chocolate production. Only the best quality cocoa beans were used in this factory.

'Where do the cocoa beans come from?' asked Rene, putting on her apron and tying back her hair for hygiene purposes.

'Originally from Mexico,' said the bossy lady, but now there are cocoa plantations in Ceylon, Java, West Africa and Brazil. Ever seen a cocoa pod? They are long and dangly and either red or yellow in colour. That's where the beans grow until they are ready for harvesting.'

'We all 'ave to listen to Maud's lecture when we arrive 'ere,' whispered one of the ladies to Rene, 'she'll tell you how the chocolate is processed next.'

I listened fascinated from beneath one of the shiny stainless steel work surfaces.

'First we tip the beans on this trundling conveyor belt and sort them by hand, picking out any irregular beans or anything that shouldn't be in there – bits of pod and stalks and so on,' continued Maud.

'Then we roast them over these giant heaters which brings out the rich flavour, the scent of which is easily recognisable as chocolate. The roasted cocoa beans 'ave a thin, papery shell around them which needs to be removed, so at this stage the beans are cracked open and the light shells are blown away with fans – a process known as winnowing – leaving behind pieces of pure cocoa bean known as 'nibs'.'

I wondered to myself whether this was where the expression 'his nibs' came from as it was popular at this time.

'The nibs are ground with stone rollers and then the full cream milk and pure refined sugar are added. The whole lot is mixed into a thick paste and then melted in giant pans whilst being constantly stirred. This is when extra cocoa butter is added. The kneading and mixing is known as 'refining' and this is a very important stage in chocolate making. This

240

is the stage we are at right now,' she stopped in front of the largest of the pans.

'Here ends the lesson,' whispered Ethel. 'We get to take home any mis-shapes,' she added.

Mmmmm, my mouth was watering. All this talk of chocolate and the overpowering scent was driving this little dog crazy.

'I don't care much for chocolate,' said the newcomer. The other women looked at Rene in amazement and disbelief.

I watched the factory women with their hair scraped off their faces and tucked away under nets, wearing white overalls or pinafores to keep their everyday clothes clean.

They were all laughing and joking as they added large quantities of ingredients to a smaller pan and swirled the mixture, releasing even more delicious sugary smells as they stirred with big wooden spoons. Every stir released a fresh burst of exciting mouth-watering aroma into the kitchen. Butter was melted, sugar was caramelised, syrup bubbled and milk was added; this was surely toffee!

A siren sounded in the factory and I forgot myself for a moment and did what comes naturally when I hear a loud noise. I started barking. There was so much noise from the hissing of the steam-powered machinery driving the conveyor belts that luckily nobody heard me.

This siren seemed to signal it was time for a tea break.

A trolley appeared at the end of the big kitchen and the factory workers turned off the gas jets under the copper pans. They swarmed around the tea trolley, jostling for a place in the queue and were still laughing and chatting as they piled sugar and milk into white china mugs which they then filled with steaming tea poured from the big shiny urn.

I could see there were also biscuits piled onto a plate.

'Mind if I have a Fig Roll?' said Rene, helping herself to a strange oblong biscuit with dark filling. I was more interested in the big pans of chocolate and toffee now cooling and unattended.

I crept out from behind the chocolate pan and edged my way to the one containing toffee.

Keeping one eye on the tea-drinking workers, I put my paws up on the side and leaned in. I just needed to lean in far enough to stick my nose into the warm toffee for a little tiny taste. Mmmmmmm.

Stealthily I got back down on all fours and crept to the chocolate pan, as if drawn by a magnet, licking my lips and hoping to repeat the tasting manoeuvre.

But this was a bigger pan and I had to get right up on the side of it and perch before I leant over, just a little bit further… just a little taste…

Splosh!

The next thing I knew I was flailing about in the molten chocolate and frantically doggy paddling to try to keep my head above the gooey brown mass which was threatening to engulf me.

The sides of the copper pan were so sheer and shiny there was no way I was going to get out! I don't usually bark when I'm trapped or lost but I did manage to let out a little whimper.

Luckily for me, tea break was over and the women quickly returned to their posts, and at once I was discovered chocolate-pawed.

''Ere, Ethel! Over 'ere. Quick…look there's some kind of animal swimming in our chocolate!' said Maud.

Thank goodness they had noticed me moving in the copper pan.

'Oh, no! We'll have to 'spoil' that batch and start all

over again,' said Ethel.

'But we haven't got time to start a new batch; management want the new sweet ready today!' reminded Maud.

Never mind that, ladies, can you please get me out?

'What is it anyway? A rat?' said another voice.

Bloomin' cheek! I thought.

'What are you doing, Maud? Be careful, it might be dangerous!'

Maud picked up a couple of tea towels and wrapped them tightly around each hand and then she leant in and hoiked me out by my tail and unceremoniously dumped me on the stainless steel work top which was meant for the cooling of confectionary.

'Why, it's a little terrier!' she said in disbelief.

I must have been quite a sight, standing there four-square and dripping puddles of chocolate which I might add was beginning to harden at an alarming rate as it cooled and set around my shaking body.

'Aw, bless 'im, 'e must have 'ad quite a fright in there, poor little chap!'

Ethel grabbed another cloth and tried to get the chocolate off me. The others soon joined in and they thought it was a huge game, all these hands chipping off the hardening chocolate shell.

Now I know what a chocolate Easter bunny feels like when children break it into little pieces!

'I wonder how he got in here,' said the newcomer Rene, looking around.

Finally they started scrubbing away at my face. Steady on ladies! This was the last straw.

'A chocolate dog! What a great idea for a novelty

246

product! We should tell management,' said Ethel.

'Nah, it'll never catch on…who would every want to eat animal-shaped chocolate?' said Maud. She went back to trying to remove my chocolate covering.

'It won't come off!' said Maud picking at my face.

''Ere let me 'ave a go,' said Ethel, setting to work vigorously with a damp cloth.

'Oh, I think that's the pattern of his face: 'e's supposed to 'ave those brown and black markings!' said a new voice. This was Beryl, obviously the more intelligent of the bunch. The ladies hooted with laughter.

'What's your name then little dog?' said Maud when my usual handsome features were restored, finally free from extra chocolate.

I couldn't tell them, but Beryl noticed my collar.

''E's got a little name tag,' she turned it over and read aloud, 'it says 'is name is Rolo!'

'Well that's a funny name, I've never heard of one

247

of them,' said Ethel. 'Our Stan 'as got one just like 'im and 'e's called Nipper, you know like the one on the record label; the little dog leaning into a gramophone.'

I heard footsteps approaching and looked towards the direction of the sound.

A man came into the kitchen at the tea trolley end wearing a flat cap and brown overall carrying a clipboard. He had a pencil stub behind his ear and an air of great self-importance.

'Now then, ladies, I hope you're not having an extended tea break,' he said.

'Uh-oh, we'd better 'ide you from Bert,' whispered Beryl and the women all stood in a row in front of me.

I sat still on the work top and started licking my paws. Ethel threw a tea towel over me. This was a great game!

'If 'e sees the little dog in 'ere, they will close the production and the launch of the new sweet will be delayed. The bosses won't be very 'appy and we won't get our bonuses!' hissed Beryl to the others.

'Larks, I need mine for one of them new-fangled vacuum cleaners,' said Maud.

'Why are you all standing about? What's going on here?' said the man looking suspiciously at the line of women standing by the cooling table.

'Nothin' Bert, we're ready for the next stage. Chocolate and toffee are both ready,' said Beryl hoping to avert attention from the work surface.

From underneath the tea towel, I heard the man telling the workers that the new moulds were ready for the chocolate to be dipped in and as soon as the chocolate set, the molten toffee would then be poured into the little chocolate buckets and a final layer of chocolate would be added to the top, sealing the toffee inside. These would then be cooled, tipped out upside down and stacked.

'What, not packed in flat trays in the usual way then?' queried Maud.

'No, the small stack will be wrapped in gold foil and covered with a paper tube. It's a new idea and cheaper than packing in boxes,' said Bert as he held up a piece of gold foil between thumb and forefinger to demonstrate. He put it down on the work surface and the foil blew onto the floor. No one seemed to notice.

'Very nice I'm sure,' said Beryl. 'What are these sweets going to be called then Bert?'

'We haven't got a name for them yet. It needs to be something short and punchy. Management are scratching their heads in a meeting right now. If they don't come up with something today the launch will be called off and you know what that means ladies.' He paused dramatically.

'Don't suppose any of you have any bright ideas?'

There was a deathly hush whilst the workers contemplated losing their bonuses and any hope of owning new electrical appliances or family holidays to the seaside, when Ethel piped up,

'What about 'Rolo'?'

The Secret Adventures of Rolo

'Brilliant,' said Maud, clapping her hands with glee.

Everyone started laughing and Bert agreed at once that it was a good catchy name and would easily fit on the wrapper and he would put it to the management straight away.

'If the 'powers that be' upstairs like the name, the design team can get to work on a brand design at once and the launch of the product won't be delayed after all. Well done, ladies,' he said.

Bert left the kitchen with his clipboard and I stayed very still under my tea towel. When he was safely out of range, the women uncovered me and made a big fuss of me, stroking me and ruffling my ears and covering me with kisses.

I thought it best to leave them at this point in case one of them tried to take me home. There was further mention of Stan and Nipper. I needed to get back to my era pronto. I bent down to retrieve the piece of gold foil.

As I journeyed through the time tunnel, I couldn't help wondering whether the first batch of Rolos

251

had any white dog hairs in them and, if they had, whether anyone had noticed. Food hygiene in the 1930s probably wasn't as strict as it is now.

The sweets were a huge success and are still packaged in the same way to this very day, proving just as popular as when they were invented.

I gave Yulia the little piece of gold foil from the packaging design and she twisted it into a dainty goblet and said she would keep it forever.

I'd like to have brought back some of the first Rolos for the smiley lady and the floppy haired boy, but how would I explain them to my people? I didn't think 80 year old chocolate would taste too good anyway. Probably be a bit white and blotchy.

'So you see, Little Pup, you have made your mark on history after all!' laughed Athelstan when I told him what had happened. But he did caution me about eating chocolate, as dogs are not supposed to eat any dairy foods for health reasons.

Later that night, curled up in my basket, I could still taste a little bit of chocolate in between the pads of my paws.

It would be another twenty years before chocolate bunnies made their first appearance at Easter and reindeers at Christmas; and to think I was the original chocolate dog!

Dog Blog #11 — According to Rolo

Today I am very excited. The smiley lady has put me in the car and off we go on a very long journey to Wales.

She tells me in the car that this is the place I was born and that it would be a little bit like going home. I can't say anything, so I stare at her as she glances at me every now and then in the rear-view mirror whilst she is driving.

We stop on the way to visit an old friend. The friend has chickens and

253

the smiley lady tells her that I am good with birds and don't chase them.

Right then, Rolo; better be on your best behaviour. They are not pigeons they are hens.

Whilst they drank their coffee, the lady said she was going to pop out to the hen house to get some fresh eggs for us to take with us.

She disappeared for ages and the smiley lady finished her coffee and started looking at her watch. She didn't want to be late for wherever it was we were heading. I started whimpering and she knew I wanted to go out.

She went to the back door and opened it for me. I ran outside and

down the garden and immediately saw
the lady had somehow shut herself
in the hen house. The hens appeared
to be laughing.

'Oh, Rolo, be a good boy and go and
fetch your mistress will you? I
can't get out!'

Instead of that, I jumped up at
the door and managed to knock
the latch, freeing the trapped
lady. She emerged bright red with
embarrassment and nearly forgot the
promised eggs.

The smiley lady patted me and gave
me a doggy treat when she heard
how I had rescued her friend. She
has no idea at all about what I am
capable of, does she?

Back in the car with the windows

255

open and the fresh air whistling
around us we continued our journey
westwards.

A white structure loomed ahead of
us. It's called the Severn Bridge.
It's very big and scary because
you can see right through it and
we have to stop at the toll booth
to pay to cross the estuary into
Wales.

The smiley lady winds down the
window and gives the man a handful
of pound coins. I bark at him. I
don't like people leaning into
our car even if they are bearing
tickets.

We pass a sign with a red dragon
on it. I think he looks a bit like
Rhydian. The sign says 'Croeso i
Cymru', which I know means 'Welcome

to Wales'.

After driving a little bit further, we see yellow signs and follow them into a car park. There are yellow banners hung above the entrance gate and on the surrounding walls with a dog with my features on the logo. This is Dog's Trust!

Wait a minute! I know the smiley lady said I was going to the Land of my Fathers but I didn't think she meant she was taking me back to the dogs' home! I started panicking.

'Surprise!' she said with glee, letting me out of the car. 'Rolo, don't look so worried; it's a dog show!'

Phew, that's all right then.

There were so many other dogs
to meet; big ones, small ones,
fluffy ones, square faced ones,
tall Greyhounds, taller Pointers,
Spaniels and Labradors and all
manner of Terriers. It was all
terribly exciting and we were eager
to greet each other. We all got
our leads tangled as we sniffed
each other politely at both ends,
anxious to introduce ourselves and
keen to make new friends.

The smiley lady led me to a table
in a marquee where they were
registering entrants for the events
of the dog show. 'Most handsome boy
dog,' she said and the registrar
wrote 'Rolo' on the list on her
clipboard, smiled and handed over a
ticket with a number.

'Listen out for the announcements

and come to the show ring when class three is called in about 20 minutes,' she said, taking the smiley lady's money.

We wandered around the stalls and the smiley lady bought me some homemade doggie treats and a new ball thrower with the Dog's Trust logo on. Lots of people stopped to admire and pat me and ask the smiley lady how old I was. I was having a lovely day out.

A voice crackled over the tanoy summoning us to the show ring. There were about 20 other so called 'handsome boy dogs' in the ring and we took our places with our owners, standing in a circle whilst the judge did her rounds. I loved listening to the soft Welsh lilt in her voice as the judge greeted each

dog in turn and asked the owners a
few questions.

When it was our turn, she said,
'Oh, handsome boyo, I must be
seeing double. I've just seen a dog
that looks exactly like you over
there!'

Now we Jack Russells are all
different types: some are quite tall
with long legs, some have short
tails and small heads, and some are
just brown or just black or like me
a mixture of the two, and we all
have different markings.

The smiley lady often laughs when
people notice the unusual swirl
on my head and she tells them that
God's hand must have slipped with
the icing bag when he was creating
me because I have a crooked line
of white from the top of my nose,
over my head, through the brown and
black markings to the white on the

The Secret Adventures of Rolo

back of my neck and the rest of my
body.
I couldn't imagine for one minute
that there was another one made
like me with a swirl on his head.
I looked across the circle where
the judge was pointing and the
smiley lady gave a little gasp.
When the parade was over and the
judge was making up her mind which
dog to award the first prize to,
the smiley lady led me across the
ring of dogs and went right up to
this counterfeit Rolo. She started
talking to the owner and I stared,
weighing up the competition.
I would say we were about the same
size and did indeed have exactly
the same pattern on our faces. I
glanced down his back and he had
the same black patches as me —
though not Shakespeare's ink spot I
hasten to add.

'Bore Da,' said a deep and gentle voice.

I peered closer at the face. His muzzle was a bit greyer than mine and his eyes didn't have quite the same shine as my chocolate drops. He seemed somehow familiar. I sniffed him around the mouth. I hear his owner say, 'This is Bryn and he is about 9 years old. He is a working dog and lives with us on our farm.'

'Is that you, son?' Bryn whispered in my ear. I could have cried. 'Dad?' I said in astonishment. 'Good to see you looking so well, son. Nice owners? Your mum will be pleased. You turned out all right then. Are you happy? They couldn't keep you and your brothers and sisters on the farm, although I

262

don't recognise your owner as the
person who came to fetch you away
from us…'

I licked him under the chin.
'I've had a few homes since then,
dad, and some different names and
I've been in and out of Dog's Trust
a few times. I live in England now,
across the bridge. I look after
this smiley lady and the floppy
haired boy. Oh, and dad… I can
time travel and I know a lot about
history and nature AND I can use a
computer and everything!'

'Still given to exaggeration then,
son?' The older dog smiled. 'We
are so proud of you, me and your
mum. Just wait till I tell her.
She won't believe I've seen you.
Don't ever forget where you came
from. Not a day goes by without her

wondering what became of you,'
'Is mum not here then?' I asked,
looking around.

'No, lad, she's had to stay home
and guard the farm.'

The two owners were still talking
about the uncanny resemblance
between us and discussing our
origins. They weren't as clever
as us and hadn't worked out the
connection.

The judge came back into the ring
and called everyone's attention.
She took the microphone and said,
'We have two handsome boy dogs and
they look so similar we couldn't
choose and so we have joint first-
place winners here today: Bryn and
Rolo.'

With that, the judge strode towards us carrying two blue rosettes. Everyone clapped and smiled. The smiley lady was in tears as she pinned the rosette on my collar and I saw my dad's owner do the same. The smiley lady took our photograph together to show the floppy haired boy how Rolo met his double, and then they disappeared into the crowd. And that was the only time I saw my father.

I was floating on a cloud of happiness and in a bit of a daze. I wished I could share it with someone.

'Come on, Rolo, let's get an ice cream,' said the smiley lady. I knew that meant she'd have the yummy bit and I'd get the end without any ice cream, but I didn't really mind.

With her tucking into her ice cream we walked to a tent where there were homeless dogs wearing coats in Dog's Trust colours saying 'take me home'. The smiley lady bent down and ruffled my ears as she gave me the end of the cone,

'Well how about it, Rolo, would you like a little playmate?'

Do you know, I'm not really sure whether I would or not.

Luckily, it was a rhetorical

question; she wasn't seriously contemplating getting a second dog. She said it was hard enough to get anyone to look after one dog when she wanted to go on holiday, and she had promised me when we went home from Dog's Trust that first time never to put me in kennels. We stood there for a while and soon she got talking to the staff in charge of rehoming. It got me thinking.

I remembered the time when I was in Dog's Trust and the smiley lady and floppy haired boy came in to choose a dog. They picked me out from the crowd because I was the only one not jumping up and down and barking. I needed to tell these dogs that their best chance of being rehomed was to act with dignity and to practice smiling up at prospective owners not barking at them. Well it worked for me, didn't it?

Whilst the smiley lady was talking I spoke to the other dogs and told them the best tactics to adopt and hopefully if they listened to what I said they would all find forever homes just like I did.

'Well how does that work?' said a Collie. 'How will we get them to notice us?'

'Yes, how do we stand out in a crowd if we don't call out?' asked an aggressive Border Terrier.

Oh dear, they just didn't get it. 'You were just lucky Rolo,' sighed a Bassett Hound with sad eyes and a tummy nearly dragging on the floor.

'I remember when you were called
Ronnie and no one wanted you,' said
a Spaniel with a hint of meanness
in his voice, 'Didn't you come back
a few times?'
I wanted to say 'well look at you;
you're still here,' but I bit my
tongue and said nothing.

You can't say I didn't try. I just
wanted all these pre-loved dogs to
find happy homes like mine. Some of
them are really nervous of other

269

dogs; some don't like men; some don't like little children. All of this depends on what experiences they had in their former homes. Rescue dogs needs lots of extra special loving and if anyone is considering getting a dog as a pet, they really should consider rehoming one rather than buying a pedigree dog.

I heard the lady from Dog's Trust telling the smiley lady that they even have a dog ambulance to rescue dogs if necessary and that adoption is all about finding the right human for the dog. As life in kennels can be quite stressful, the staff try to make life there as interesting and stimulating as possible. The smiley lady said they did a wonderful job. Nearly 15,000 dogs were rehomed by Dog's Trust in the previous year.

I used to think that the saying:
'You can't teach an old dog new
tricks' was right.

Well, actually you can. I'm proof
of that. I came to the smiley lady
with very little training; I just
needed to learn the house rules.
That reminded me of Britain's Got
Talent again. I wonder what the
floppy haired boy had in mind for
our act.

Time to go home and I slept for
most of the long journey.
I thought it was funny that we
didn't have to pay a toll to cross
the scary bridge when we left
Wales; I was all geared up for
another bark at the person in the
ticket booth.

I was very proud of my 'handsome

271

dog' rosette and the smiley lady pinned it up on the noticeboard in the kitchen so I can see it when I go to bed.

Now I know exactly where I get my good looks from. I wondered where my dad's rosette had been displayed and was trying to picture him in a Welsh farmhouse telling my mum all about meeting their youngest son...

The Secret Adventures of Rolo

Chapter 14

Rolo and the Willow Pattern

I'd been thinking for some time about the missing number five on the sundial on the church. There was only one thing for it – I would have to work out a way of being there at 5 o'clock to see what happens during the hour when the shadow hits the gap on the clock.

But then I thought that with it being winter there would be no sun to cast a shadow at that hour – it was either too early in the morning or too late in the afternoon for the sun to be high enough in the sky to cast a shadow at all; that's assuming that there is even going to be any sun on a particular day!

5pm would be difficult for me, because although I'm often in the vicinity of the church at that time I am usually on the end of the lead, attached to the smiley lady enjoying my late afternoon walk by the river.

5am would be easier for me as I am generally returning from my secret night time adventures about then and sneaking back into my basket in good time before the kitchen door opens and the smiley lady lets me out into the garden.

But now in winter it would be dark at both 5am and 5pm. The thought did occur to me that the sundial may have been installed in winter and therefore the installers thought they didn't need a five, but no that was just silly.

I wondered what might happen if I took a torch and shone a light onto the dial imitating the sun's rays – that might do the trick.

As luck would have it, the next afternoon the smiley lady took a phone call and went to meet a friend at a Christmas market in a nearby town and the floppy haired boy took the opportunity of going round to a friend's house, so I would have the chance to run down to the church without them knowing.

They told me to be a good boy for a couple of hours and bribed me with a biscuit.

I had to nip upstairs first to the floppy haired boy's bedroom as I was fairly sure he had a little torch there that you could strap to your head. Luckily he had left the door open and his room was in its usual state of mess.

I rummaged around a bit and fortunately found the torch under the bed and it fitted me perfectly. He had strapped it on me once when we were playing and I think that was probably the last time it was used.

A quick scout around to make sure that the house really was empty and I glanced up at the kitchen clock. It was already after half past four. I would have to get a move on.

I approached the kitchen sink, pulled open the cupboard door with my right paw, barged past the cleaning products and tugged the trapdoor ring. I didn't have any time to lose as I didn't know how long my people would be out for, and I had to use my secret terrier escape hatch under the fence as I ran down the road to the church as fast as my little legs would carry me.

A few prowling cats were surprised to see me running away from the house on my own at this time of day, but I didn't have time to chase them and ignored their taunts.

'What have you got on your head, Rolo? Going mining?' I could hear them sniggering behind their paws. I'd get them later.

There was a definite chill in the air and greyness and that smell of damp that only comes towards the end of November.

I reached the churchyard and sat down heavily on the gravel path, panting with the exertion and excitement of the afternoon run, and then using my paw, switched on the lamp on my head.

My aim was to position myself so as to imitate the sun's shadow hitting the spindle of the sun dial.

I had to move a few times to find the right place to create a directional beam. Was it 5 o'clock yet, I wondered? I glanced up at the church clock and indeed it was, right on the hour.

The light beam shone out. The shadow hit the gap where the five should be.

Nothing happened.

I felt a bit foolish sitting there on the path shining a light on the sundial and was pleased no one was around to see.

I switched the lamp off and removed the head torch, leaving it in the church porch.

It was then that I noticed a box of bric-a-brac left on the floor by the big wooden door.

Further investigation revealed cake plates and cups and saucers, probably left for church afternoon teas.

A large blue and white oval plate caught my eye, as it stuck out from the box, and it seemed to draw me towards it.

I approached the box of crockery and sniffed the plate suspiciously, thinking it must have once been a carving platter. I started thinking about all the roasting joints it must have seen – Sunday roast dinner usually meant a bone for me – and all at once I felt a bit funny and I found the scene on the plate getting nearer and nearer.

277

Either I had become much smaller or the plate had grown! It was drawing me towards it like a powerful magnet. The next thing I knew I was inside the scene on the plate.

Glancing around I seemed to be in a Chinese ornamental garden with symmetrical fences and neatly manicured hills.

Small people with their hair plaited in single pigtails and wearing patterned silk pyjamas were running across a wooden bridge and they were all carrying boxes of some kind. They seemed to be in a hurry.

I ran after them, barking to attract their attention

but they didn't take any notice of me. I wondered if they could even see me. Was I even really there?

I peered down into the water to see fish darting about amongst the weed beneath the lily pads. Leaning in I saw a reflection of a little dog staring back.

The weirdest thing of all was that everything in this place was made up of just two colours: blue and white. How odd, I thought.

My Terrier curiosity got the better of me and I decided to explore this scene further.

There were a few buildings dotted around and a couple of pagodas, and the trees were in miniature – bonsai trees and neatly tamed flowering sumacs. It felt like late spring in this magical place. One small tree was in full blossom, possibly a cherry tree as the air was filled with a sweet scent. I resisted the urge to raise my leg against the trunk – I didn't want to break the charm of this idyllic setting.

The hurrying pigtailed people had disappeared and across the water I could see an island with another pagoda on it.

In the clear blue sky above, two dark blue birds flew, playing chase with each other and darting and swooping through the candy floss white fluffy clouds.

More movement. A boat was coming into view, perhaps from the island; it looked like it had little houses on top of it.

I went down to the water's edge and bent down for a cooling drink and all at once a storm came from nowhere and the water stirred and swelled and suddenly became a seething choppy mass.

Pitter-patter, pitter-patter: the rain fell heavily, splotches on the ground joining up and spoiling the scene.

The blue birds circled frantically overhead, and the downpour caused the white cherry blossom to be dashed to the ground and the entire blue and white background started to run.

The scene was diluting and everything was

smudging!

I ran back across the bridge and into the nearest pagoda to shelter from the rain. The building was blurring around me. I knew I had to get out of here fast!

The horizon had vanished, the tree had disappeared and now water covered the whole landscape, rising by the second. If I stayed much longer I would surely be washed away!

Suddenly I found myself back in the church porch, and I glanced down and noticed blue paw prints on the flagstone floor. The ladies who cleaned the church so thoroughly every week wouldn't be very pleased! I picked up the abandoned torch in my teeth.

I had lost all sense of time and had no idea how long this episode had lasted. I had a quick look up at the sundial to check the time, but of course it was too dark to see. I put the lamp on my head and turned on my torch and shone the beam on the hands of the church clock which told me it was nearly 6 o'clock.

I would have to get a move on because the smiley lady might be opening the front door at any moment and would expect to be greeted by a waggy tail.

I ran all the way home without chasing any cheeky cats or foraging squirrels, who were busily gathering in their winter store of nuts.

Back home, I settled happily in my basket and licked my blue paws clean, pleased to have got away with my exciting adventure. I had no idea how I had entered the scene on the plate. Was it something to do with the missing 'V' on the sundial or was that just a coincidence? Had I simply imagined the whole adventure?

I heard a key turn in the lock and ran to greet the smiley lady by putting my paws up on her legs and burrowing into her coat. She ruffled my ears and then said,

'Oh Rolo, where has all this come from?' as she pushed my legs aside, telling me to get down.

Looking up at her coat I saw the tell-tale blue paw prints. I followed her into the kitchen avoiding eye contact and slunk into my basket. She rummaged under the sink for a cloth to clean the paw marks off her coat, wondering out loud where the bucket had gone.

I glanced up at the calendar hanging on the kitchen door.

It was the last day of November. Something stirred in my little doggy brain, the memory of an earlier conversation.

Postscript

Meanwhile in a disused quarry on the edge of the forest, a white dragon was growing bigger and stronger every day.

His wings were stretching and he was keen to get outside to test them away from the confines of his cave. The woodland folk were struggling to keep him inside and explained their concerns to Athelstan.

One evening Yulia and Da settled Gwyn on his nest for the night, having brought him his supper of wild rabbits. Unbeknown to them, whilst they were fussing around the hatchling, a stranger entered the cave and waited patiently for the woodland folk to leave.

Yellow eyes glinted in the darkest corner, causing Gwyn to flap his wings frantically in alarm, hoping to bring back his nursemaids.

'The time for adventure is coming, Gwyn,' said Rhydian. 'Be patient.'

The Secret Adventures of Rolo

285